Julie eagerly maneuvered around the stick ___ and shaped herself to straddle Sheila's lap. Her hands locked around Sheila's waist, gripped her, pulled her close. Sheila's back arched instantly, sandwiching Julie against the dashboard, then released and arched again . . . quickly finding the familiar rhythm between them. Julie's head dropped back as Sheila's fingers peeled her jeans into a tight tangle around her knees, then opened her . . . slid in easily, deeply . . . She felt warmer and more liquid with each push of Sheila's body against hers, and rose quickly to the brink of orgasm. But she held back . . . riding its crest effortlessly and without frustration . . . knowing that her growing tension and sensitivity was every bit as delightful as the final spasm that would soon rock through her.

DEVOTION

WRITTEN BY

MINDY KAPLAN

THE NAIAD PRESS, INC.
1995

Printed in the United States of America on acid-free paper
First Edition

Edited by Karin Kallmaker
Cover design by Bonnie Liss (Phoenix Graphics)
Typeset by Sandi Stancil

Library of Congress Cataloging-in-Publication Data

Kaplan, Mindy, 1961 –
    Devotion / by Mindy Kaplan.
        p.   cm.
    ISBN 1-56280-093-0
    I. Title.
PS3561.A5637D48   1995
813'.54—dc20
                                                            94-43822
                                                            CIP

The tradition of opening books with dedications is surely a gift to the author. There's no more profound privilege than the chance to voice one's love, respect, appreciation ... perhaps even devotion, to those people, past and present, who have fanned the fires of our inspiration and, without exception or apology, pointed us toward our own courage. Such teachers come in many forms and my life has, thankfully, been full of them. And so I dedicate this first work to the "A-list" of characters who have guided me through the turning points of my own story.

Doc — whose expectations were always just high enough to make me jump

Mary Cochran — who kicked my butt out of the closet

Lisa Kaplan — who taught me to beat the odds by overlooking them

Tallu Rosen — who showed me the world and freed me to find my place in it

Doris Kaplan — who's love was always profuse and unconditional

Lucia Weinhardt — who always adds zash to the brew of life

Carol Aff — who reigns as the queen of everything, freeing me up for other things

Carol McGinnis — whose fundamental silliness keeps me sane

Megan Rutherford — who never-ever-ever lets my emperor keep his clothes

With deepest love and gratitude to:

Arlene Battishill (my little engine that could), who traveled eight years by my side planting seeds that will continue to grow

and

Cathy Robertson, who electrifies me with the fire of her heart and lets me be the only raptor

Acknowledgments

My heartfelt thanks to:

Niara Modi, Mario Araya, Fran Dunaway, Lisa King, Emily Decker, Robyn Du Boff, Sue Iskenderian, Barbara Grier, Pam Kuri, and Karin Kallmaker — who lent their tremendous energy toward the creation of this project in its many aspects:

Jan Derbyshire, Kate Twa, Cindy Girling, Eileen Barrett, and Steve Adams — who blessed me with their faith and talent

Ruben, Barry, Ken, Jeff and Rob — the gentlemen who stand beside me and fill my spirit

Special Acknowledgment

To Emily Saliers and Amy Ray — praise from a stranger, for setting me straight so many times when I went crooked.

About the Author

Mindy Kaplan is Philadelphia born, Miami reared, and currently enamored by the mountains and water of Vancouver, where she works as a writer/director. She has a doctoral degree in clinical psychology, and practiced therapy for several years before deciding to become downwardly mobile. She served a stint as a professor at Central Michigan University, where she founded and became first director of the Office of Gay and Lesbian Programs. In that position, she produced a documentary/educational video about homophobia and the experiences of lesbian and gay students. The year-long project reignited an old dream of filmmaking, and inspired a major career transition (from having one to not).

Her first screenplay, a ten-minute short called "Meeting Dad," won a Gold Award at the 1993 Houston International Film Festival. During that time, she also developed and wrote "Investi-Gator"™, an animated TV series for kids. The show, which has an educational bent, is currently being marketed to raise financing for production. *Devotion* was project number three, and number four is anybody's guess.

The Players . . .

Jan Derbyshire

KATE TWA

CINDY GIRLING

Northern Arts Entertainment presents **Devotion** an *Auntie Em Production*
Produced by Arlene Battishill   Written and Directed by Mindy Caplan.

I'm going to kill myself!" Julie Rosen hung upside down on the couch, tossing kernels of Jiffy Pop into the air and catching them in her mouth. She reached for an escapee, inadvertently rubbing paint from her splattered overalls onto the chintz upholstery. "Turpentine . . ." she mumbled, scratching at it with her thumbnail. "Oh, nothing . . ." She switched the phone to her other ear and made a mental note that forest green looked good against ecru.

"I wait by the phone for you all day!" She covered the obstinate smudge with a throw pillow and flicked the TV remote. "Every day!" Dionne Warwick's Psychic Hotline was on — her favorite infomercial. Late-night TV was reliable in that way.

"I'm pining away for you. What are you doing?" She ran her hand along the base of the couch. The wood needed refinishing. Maybe after she got off the phone . . .

"Packing?" She twisted upright, jet black hair tumbling and curling around smooth, tawny shoulders. "You unpacked?" She pulled her hair back into a ponytail. "You never unpack when you're here . . . and you know how much Stella hates that!" She poked a socked foot at Stella, dachshund extraordinaire, who gobbled brazenly from the popcorn bowl. "Personally, I'm fine with it . . ."

In her pause, Julie could hear the wind skimming down from Lion's Head Mountain, whose peak still clung to its late spring snow. A slight chill passed through the open glass doors, as the cliff's cool breath crossed the bay, dark from the absent moon, and greeted the rocky shoreline. Wind chimes resonated in rich reply, like a familiar lover. Julie switched off the TV and focused on their melody. "Yeah, I miss you too. So . . . when are we getting married?" She twirled a dark curl between two fingers, chuckled. "Does it get cold in hell?"

Across the continent, in a motel room that smelled like truck exhaust, Sheila Caston bounced on her stuffed suitcase. "Okay, okay." Phone in one hand, convenience store coffee in the other, she balanced precariously at the edge of the bed.

"I, Sheila, take you, Julie . . . to bed every night? And I thought you loved me for my mind." She dumped another sugar packet into the Styrofoam cup and swallowed the cold remains. "Nope, no coffee before bed." She tossed the cup across the room, hitting the mirror and missing the garbage can. Softball was more her game than basketball . . . and it *would've* been a fair pitch.

"Love you too." She hopped down from the bed, latched the suitcase shut, thought of the damp curls that wound along the base of Julie's neck when they made love. "Honey . . ." She stared into the darkness, caught her reflection in the window. She'd been mistaken for k.d. lang again today, but all she saw was a tired woman far from home. "I miss you" was what she felt. "Goodnight" was what she said.

Julie watched the city come to life as she wound the blue Fiat through the brisk morning. Top down, gloves and heater on, she raced the approaching ferry to the port . . . a game she enjoyed, knowing it stood no chance of beating her. She smoothed some ChapStick over her lips, grabbed the Drakkar Noir from the glovebox and rubbed a drop between her wrists. Melissa Etheridge blasted louder than the wind.

Always lucky with parking, she pulled into a spot beside the arrival deck as a busy troop secured the ship. She yanked the bandanna from her hair, tied it around her neck, and positioned herself by the

concession stand with an "I've-been-here-for-hours" look. A buzzing crowd poured onto the pier. Backpackers and businessmen, looking more like each other every day. Kids, dogs, cyclists, and at last, Sheila.

They hugged each other hugely and held each other tight. Sheila took a step back and looked Julie up and down, deeply thankful that this port and this woman meant home. Smiling, Julie pulled off a glove and raised her palm perpendicular to her face. Sheila completed the playful ritual ... poking two fingers toward Julie's eyes, a la Three Stooges. She took Julie's hand, kissed it with a sly half-grin. "We've got four hours ..."

Julie grabbed Sheila's suitcase and tugged her toward the car. "I'll drive fast!"

The ride home was interrupted by a pull-off into Lion's Bay Park, down the side road marked "maintenance vehicles only." Julie still had her decal from last summer, when she'd worked on the landscaping crew, and she knew they could park by the isolated lagoon without problem. Besides, Sheila's hands had been traveling her body since the moment they'd left the port, and Julie was ready five miles ago to feel Sheila inside her.

She pulled down to the water's edge, shut off the motor but kept the tape deck powered. Music was important and Melissa Etheridge proved as scorching in the bright afternoon as she always had in the dark envelope of night.

Julie eagerly maneuvered around the stick shift and shaped herself to straddle Sheila's lap. Her hands locked around Sheila's waist, gripped her ass, pulled her close. Sheila's back arched instantly, sandwiching

Julie against the dashboard, then released and arched again . . . quickly finding the familiar rhythm between them. Julie's head dropped back as Sheila's fingers peeled her jeans into a tight tangle around her knees, then opened her . . . slid in easily, deeply . . . till they pressed against her cervix. She felt warmer and more liquid with each push of Sheila's body against hers, and rose quickly to the brink of orgasm. But she held back . . . riding its crest effortlessly and without frustration . . . knowing that her growing tension and sensitivity was every bit as delightful as the final spasm that would soon rock through her.

Sheila felt a slowing of Julie's breath . . . a slight adjustment of Julie's body against her hand . . . She understood the language, and readily joined in prolonging the pleasure by waiting. A dividend program, of sorts, which Julie had introduced her to the first time they'd made love. "The less chips you cash in at once," Julie had explained, "the longer you get to play." Ever the ambitious student, Sheila studied the lesson long and hard — perfecting the fundamentals, experimenting with variations. She still felt amazed and lucky as hell for finding such intense pleasure with someone she adored so much.

Julie's scent was heady, intoxicating like the deep of the forest surrounding them, and Sheila felt seized by a kind of dizziness that unraveled all rational thought into pure desire. She buried a third finger deep between Julie's legs, then a fourth. Julie's hands took hold of her hair, pulling their mouths together in a bacchanalian revelry of lips and teeth and tongue.

Their movements quickened by degree, becoming stronger, more deliberate, until Sheila felt a sudden

7

stiffening of Julie's body and knew release was imminent. She slid her thumb back and forth along the stem of Julie's clitoris, imagined it was her tongue instead ... crossing, dipping, pressing, tasting ...

And when Sheila could no longer resist the rhythmic push of her lover's pelvis against her own, she called Julie's name ... and they surged together, submitting finally to the pleas of their hungry flesh and cashing their chips with a vengeance.

Sweaty and filled with a sense of well-being, they wrapped together and slipped into the opacity of sleep under the afternoon sun.

Cigarette smoke rose through cones of colored light and gathered into a wispy haze along the ceiling's edge. Votive candles flickered in logoed shot glasses. Julie made her way to the front of the club, knowing Katie would be waiting at their usual table, stage left.

They kissed hello, signaled for a waiter and dug out the free drink tickets stashed beneath the ashtray. Julie ordered a half-carafe of Riesling and pulled out her Marlboros. Katie got a mineral water and studied Julie's cigarettes, vacillating between longing and resoluteness. She silently recited her daily affirmation, reminding herself that pregnancy and smoking didn't match. Some people thought pregnancy didn't match Katie in general, but she knew they were wrong.

Katie's struggle was evident, and Julie crushed the just-lit cigarette into the ashtray. "Sorry."

"So, what do you think she's doing?" Katie grabbed Julie's wrist, checked her glow-in-the-dark watch.

Julie noted the time. "Playing with her teeth . . ." She chuckled.

A puzzled Katie watched the last wisp of blue smoke curl toward the stagelights.

Red chattering-teeth hopped through a crowd of wind-up toys along the cluttered dressing room table. "Wanna come back to my place and floss?" Sheila joked to no one in particular, alone in the room. Sheila joked well. Sheila joked always. It usually got her by.

"Hey Sheila," came the familiar call through the door. "Two minutes!"

"I'll be there!" She tousled her bangs, which routinely conquered palmsful of gel to hang in her eyes, and clipped on her suspenders. She glanced at the photograph wedged crookedly in the mirror frame. Julie in the claw-foot tub . . . surrounded by candles . . . buried in bubbles . . .

She looked forward to getting the show over with and going home with her lover.

"JULIE! JULIE!" Voices screeched in greeting and

laughter, as a motley female triumvirate filed toward Julie and Katie's table. Jane arrived first, her long chestnut hair wrapped wildly around her five foot frame. "Thanks for the invite!" She locked Julie in a hug. "Been missing you big time."

"Good to see you too, Rock Star!" Julie gave her a tight squeeze.

"I ditched the band in Toledo!" Jane announced proudly. "Told 'em to take the night off and meet me tomorrow in Indianapolis." She swung her hair back and gestured east. "Fifty-three days, forty-eight gigs."

"Forty-eight gigs, forty-*nine* groupies," Sharon quipped under her breath, then leaned to kiss Julie. "Ask her about the twins in DC," she whispered.

"Over cocktails." Julie smiled. "So how's politics."

Sharon looked heavenward. "Every time I think we're getting somewhere, there's an election and poof! Start over!"

"She does it for the parties!" Michelle leaned across the table, her burgundy outfit draped sensuously across ebony skin. "She was at the White House last month. Who ever would've thought..."

"This is gorgeous." Julie stroked Michelle's sleeve. "One of yours, I assume."

Michelle nodded. "Fall line, last year's."

Jane straddled a chair. "I'm thinkin' about orderin' a line for the band. Maybe somethin' in black..." She winked at Julie. "Whaddaya think?"

"Novel..." Sharon gibed, unable to remember the last time she'd seen Jane in anything *but* black.

Jane dismissed the comment with a flick of her wrist, impressed that Sharon had at least managed not to blurt out anything about the twins yet.

"Settle, ladies . . ." Michelle admonished. "I don't think Julie asked us here to listen to this."

"On the contrary." Julie put her arm around Michelle. "It's one of my greatest pleasures."

"You've seen her on national television, making those talk show hosts squirm in their seats . . ."

The women scrambled to arrange themselves around the table, as the emcee's voice boomed over the loudspeaker and the lights dimmed.

"And now, back in her home town, on her opening night here at Punchlines Comedy Club, please welcome . . . Sheila Caston!"

Enthusiastic applause beckoned Sheila to the stage, a welcome suitor. People always thought it "took guts" to be a performer, but Sheila found comfort in the spotlight's protective glare. Interminably dashing and effervescent, she'd amassed a faithful following over the years. These days, even her open lesbianism had become a commodity . . . providing trendy anecdotes for her routines.

"Hello, you crazy folks!" Sheila grabbed the microphone from its stand. "It's great to be back home!" She paced the stage, acknowledging the gracious welcome. "I just finished a tour of some of the finer red-neck regions of North America. You know the places . . . where nine out of ten people are literally afraid to drink homo milk." She smiled. "They won't even drink two-percent, in case fifty of them are in a room together!" She eyed the crowd suspiciously, as if figuring out who it might be. "Well, home crowd . . . what shall we talk about tonight?"

"Intimacy!" came a call from the side of the room.

Sheila shook like she'd never heard something so frightening. "Intimacy, huh?" She turned to address the female heckler. "Don't I know you? Aren't you in my group therapy ... Tuesdays and Thursdays? And Wednesdays ... and Sundays ..." She sported her suavest lounge singer expression and broke into song. "Are the stars out tonight ... I don't know if it's cloudy or bright ... 'cause I only have eyes, for ..." She slowly scanned the crowd. "Well ... most of you really!" She chuckled along with the audience. "No ... for you!" She pointed to a young woman near the front. "Do you drink milk?"

"Homo milk!" The retort came with a white-toothed smile.

"Ladies and Gentlemen ..." Sheila pointed to the woman. "My next lover!" She took a long pause, stared out at the crowd. "Well, that certainly made a few people sit up in their seats and have a good look around. Are we in the right club, Marge? Is this lesbian poet night? If it was, I could read you a few selections from my chapbook." She cleared her throat and extended her hands before her, as if holding a book. Her tone was serious, deadpan. "Fuck men." She paused, then grinned. "I don't think so! But you know ... it never ceases to amaze me, whenever an audience finds out I'm a lesbian, the same thing happens." She glanced around, pointed to a straight couple up front. "See this!" The couple squirmed slightly and leaned closer together. "The guys always move right up next to their wives or

13

girlfriends . . . put a big strong arm around them. Like they're protecting them from something! Oooh . . . beware the pull of the Lesbo Magnet!" She reached toward the woman like a hypnotist. "You're getting closer . . . closer . . ."

The woman flashed a smile, which Sheila took as a measure of success. She'd brought down a small barrier, made one more person less afraid. The choice to be "out" had been encouraged by Katie, who'd been her manager since the earliest days back at the "C-level" clubs. She hadn't truly needed a manager until recently, but Katie's friendship had been the singular constant along her winding ascent.

Squinting through the spotlight glare, Sheila searched stage left for Katie and Julie. She often turned to them to ground herself during shows, sometimes forgetting they weren't there when she was on the road. But she was home. They would be there.

"Whoa! A blast from my past." Sheila's eyes settled on the familiar faces of her friends seated around the table. "I see my manager has planted a few of my old friends in the audience to make sure I get a few laughs." She waved. "Hi, girls." Raucous hellos and waves came back at her.

From the darkness in the back of the room, Lynn Webster looked on — a stunning sentry. Aquamarine eyes, as penetrating as they were impenetrable. Blonde hair pulled up and back to match the sleek tailored lines of her Armani suit. Emerald earrings, her casual ones, square cut, flanked by small, tasteful diamonds. A smile that made you forget your own name and not care.

"I wish it was this easy to meet women." Sheila motioned to the "homo milk woman," a name she would fondly use later when referring to the beauty who'd heckled her. "But it isn't! Is it girlfriends?"

The crowd conceded a resounding "no."

"And you know why . . . ?" Sheila donned a serious countenance. "Because lesbians are cool. Oh yeah. We're extremely cool." She fought back a grin. "If we wanted to meet someone, we'd never just go up to them and look them straight in the eye. No, that would be far too simple."

Knowing chuckles spread through the room.

"You see, what we like to do is . . ." She positioned herself center stage, stood stiff and motionless. "Okay . . ." She swept her eyes slowly left, right, left again.

The audience erupted in laughter.

"It's ridiculous, you know! I mean, how are we supposed to meet someone if we can't look at them? That's why, if a lesbian says she's seeing someone, she's serious." Sheila feigned excitement, her voice playfully mocking. "Really? You're seeing someone? You mean, like, right in the eye?"

The crowd howled.

"And that's why, if you're a lesbian, anonymous sex means sleeping with someone who hasn't dated at least six of your closest personal friends." She looked over toward her comrades and pretended to count them. Julie pointed a tell-tale finger at Michelle, who pointed at Jane, who pointed at Sharon. Safe from accusation, Katie enjoyed the fray.

"Intimacy . . . AHHHHHH!" Sheila shook from head to toe, regained her composure. "Don't get me wrong. I love intimacy. The little touches . . . the sweet kisses . . . the breath on breath . . . It's that other stuff I can't handle. Stuff like . . . truth, vulnerability, and that big word . . . that big, bad word . . . mahogany!" She paused for sweeping laughter and applause. "Ah yes. Ladies and Gentlemen . . ." She motioned to the wooden stool beside her. "My next lover!" She bent, kissed it, gave it two knocks for luck.

Julie rolled her eyes and smiled. For all her bravado, Sheila was firmly rooted in their relationship and both of them knew it. In fact, it had usually been Julie's own lifestyle that caused problems in her relationships. The hours she put in at the gallery . . . prefaced and followed by the hours in her studio at home. Past lovers had accusingly referred to her as a "free spirit," throwing epithets like "self-sufficient," "self-reliant," "self-contained," as if the word "self" was *itself* a bad word. And, when challenged, Julie could deftly argue whichever angle of the independent vs. interdependent vs. codependent polemic suited her purpose at that moment. But she and Sheila had never trodden that path. With Sheila on the road so much, Julie's "self-sufficiency" went unchallenged, was even reinforced. And that worked just fine for her, except on those occasional days when she could have used a hug, and those nights when the bed seemed too big without Sheila there and the wind chimes sang a song they could have made love to . . .

Julie leaned back in her chair, sipped her wine, watched her girlfriend work the room.

"Let's talk about old flames, shall we?" Sheila leaned to address an older man at one of the front tables. "I bet we've had a few of the same, sir. Have you ever had a crush on a movie star?"

The gentleman nodded his head and smiled.

"Yeah, me too. When I was a kid I had it BAD for Julie Andrews..."

Snickers rippled through the crowd.

"Come on... I'm not alone, am I? I would have even been one of those goofy von Trapp kids just to be close to her... to watch her picking edelweiss..." Sheila plucked several imaginary flowers from the air and waved them under her nose. "Of course, as I grew older, my fantasy evolved... into something... completely twisted..." She pulled her suspenders forward and let them snap back against her, then reassumed her lounge singer pose and broke into song to the tune of "My Favorite Things."

"Hot sweaty bodies in warm summer weather... You strapped to my bed frame in chains and black leather... Ice cubes, hot candle wax, hanging in slings..." She raised her arms to the audience. "Everybody!" She conducted wildly as the room filled with song. "These are a few of my favorite things!"

She waited for the roar to die down. That one always got a huge response, and she was big on audience participation. Another happy accident she'd discovered, a tool for disarming even the most recalcitrant spectator. She never pulled punches, but always tried to deliver them as punchlines.

"Ah, straight women, the truly unattainable..."

17

She shook her head, feigning grief. "Ooh baby, hurt me! I love you so much it doesn't even hurt when you hurt me." She rocked her shoulders back and forth, as if being hit by bullets that bounced off and fell to the ground. "Ping! Ping! Ping!"

Knowing hoots and howls burst from the dykes in the crowd. Hadn't everyone once fallen in love with a straight best friend, a co-worker, brother's girlfriend?

"So, I'm not the only one in therapy here, am I?" She chuckled. Her own on-again off-again venture onto the proverbial couch had provided abundant grist for her comedy mill. "You'd love my therapist . . . Dr. Been-There-Done-That. There's no shocking that old girl!" Sheila shook her head. "The first seven years, all we talked about were the feelings associated with unrequited love. You've got obsession, temptation, infatuation, anticipation, elation . . . And what do all these words have in common?" She paused, paced, paused. "They all end in 'shun'!" She snickered. "Well thanks a lot, Doc! Here . . ." She dug into her pockets, pulling out imaginary riches. "Take the keys to my car . . . my house . . . I don't need to eat." She stared proudly at the invisible treasures piled before her. "The next eight years were dedicated entirely to this ground-breaking concept . . . Tragedy plus time equals comedy." She reached again into her pockets. "Well here, take my boat, please. No really, you deserve it way more than me!" She checked her watch. "And speaking of therapy, I see my time is up."

Sheila returned to center stage and slipped the microphone back in its stand. "Well, you've been an audience . . ." She chuckled. "No, you've been a *great* audience, and I'd like to invite you all out for a drink on me!" She glanced charmingly at Katie. "My manager hates when I do that."

Accustomed to Sheila's antics, Katie rolled her hazel eyes and nodded at the crowd.

"The women's club is just down the street, and for you ladies with male partners . . ." Sheila scanned the room, smiled slyly . . . "The boys' club is right next door."

An amused groan rose from the men in the crowd, as their wives and girlfriends poked at them teasingly.

"Spread out, expand your horizons, meet later for pizza. It'll be a good time!" She bowed in response to the gracious applause. "Thanks for coming out and supporting live comedy. I'm Sheila Caston. Goodnight."

♥ ♥ ♥

"I can't believe you guys are here!" Sheila escorted her friends through the maze of backstage hallways. "I could barely get through my act!"

"She's to blame." Sharon swung her blonde mane back and motioned toward Julie.

"Yeah," Michelle chimed in. "We tried to get out of it, but she bribed us with plane tickets, front row seats . . ."

"The promise of beautiful women," Jane interjected coyly.

Julie shrugged her shoulders. "It's true."

Sheila pulled Julie close. Where past lovers had interfered with her friendships, Julie facilitated them. She kissed her on the cheek. "Thanks," she whispered.

As they hugged, Julie noticed an envelope sticking

out from under the dressing room door. She stooped to pick it up. "Your fans are getting rather aggressive," she joked.

"More letters from the lesbian lovelorn." Katie pushed the door open and winked.

"More?" Michelle was titillated. Julie motioned toward a stack of envelopes on the table, which Michelle eagerly seized and inspected. "Can we read them?"

Sheila made a playful grab for the letters. "No way!"

"She's embarrassed," Julie explained.

"Around us?" Jane pouted. "You must be kidding."

Michelle held out the envelopes, taunting. "Oh, come on."

"We promise we won't laugh . . ." Sharon appealed, innocent-faced. "Too hard!"

Realizing the futility of her protest, Sheila slumped back on the couch as Michelle handed out the letters. Sharon tore hers open first. "Dear Sheila, I've never written a letter like this before, but I felt as though I had to. My psychic told me that we were destined to be together . . ."

Sheila elbowed Julie. "Wonder what your psychic would say about that?"

Julie pondered with a smile.

"Dear Sheila," Michelle began. "I've recently ended a long-term relationship. I know this may sound crazy, but after seeing you the first time, I knew that I wanted to be with you . . ."

"Women in transition," Sheila quipped. "A specialty of mine!"

"Now, this one's pretty nice..." Jane offered. "Dear Sheila, I've really enjoyed watching your shows. I've seen you eight times now..."

Sheila leaned to look at the letter. "I love this woman."

"If you're ever in Atlanta," Jane continued, "you're welcome to... share my futon."

Surrounded by ten raised eyebrows, Sheila made light. "Happens all the time!" She shrugged.

Julie mustered her best dirty look.

"The offer, I mean."

The room was silent.

"Whoa!" Sheila jumped to her feet. "That's enough adoration for one night. Are you guys coming over?"

A unanimous "yes" spurred the group out the door. Katie grabbed the pile of unopened envelopes and carried them along.

The women laughed and carried on like teenagers as they piled out of Katie's van and traveled the short path to the beach house. Katie walked backwards, addressing the group. "I couldn't believe it! She said if I'd introduce her to Sheila, she'd make it worth my while!" Katie glanced down at her eight-months-pregnant belly and shrugged. "It obviously never occurs to anyone that I might be *straight.*"

Sheila suffered a momentary lapse into political correctness. "Well, lesbians do have kids, you know."

"It's guilt by association," Michelle teased.

Katie poked her. "That's a bunch of crap." She

really didn't mind people thinking she was gay, she just believed no assumptions should be made about anyone's sexuality.

"Well..." Sheila batted her eyelashes. "There's always hope!" She was relieved to find herself once again politically impaired. Or was it politically challenged...?

Stella barked and spun in excited circles as the group filed into the foyer. Visitors were always an excellent source of attention.

"Sit down, girl!" Sheila implored. "Come on... sit!"

Stella romped joyously, oblivious to Sheila's commands. Her tiny claws tapped brightly against the black and white tile. Katie mumbled casually on her way down the hall, "Have a seat, Stella."

Stella sat and watched lovingly as Katie disappeared into the living room. Sheila stared down at her, shook her head. "Thanks pal."

Stella barked and spun in a circle, demanding final say.

Sheila grimaced, but secretly admired the feistiness of her ever-underfoot companion. After all, Stella was the first pet she'd ever had. Her parents had always kept cats around, and the truth was, she was allergic to them... a fact which, as a lesbian, she obviously could never admit. She'd periodically weighed the pros and cons of pet parenting, but it had always seemed like too much of a commit-ment... until a guest at their last Halloween party discovered five-week-old Stella curled under some driftwood behind the house, and Julie took her in "just for the night." They'd posted signs around the neighborhood and placed ads in the paper, but within days they were both secretly hoping no one would call. No one did, and Katie threw them a baby shower.

With the sliding glass doors open, the sound of rolling waves advanced into the living room and through the house. Julie hit the answering machine button and began lighting candles as everyone settled in. The first message was from Megan, who'd interviewed Sheila several years prior for a local cable show and had been a friend ever since.

"Hey you guys, it's me. Give me a buzz when you get in . . . or maybe I'll see you later at the club."

"Yes you will." Sheila smiled to herself in the kitchen, happy to be entertaining and surrounded by friends.

Beep. "Hello, Sheila. This is Bill Matthews from Mirage Television Productions in L.A."

The unfamiliar voice caught Sheila's attention.

"We've secured financing to produce a pilot episode for a sit-com, and we've got some network interest in picking up the show, and . . . what else?"

Sheila pulled her head out of the refrigerator, curious. "Oh yeah, we'd like you to consider the lead role. That is, if you're interested." Bill chuckled.

All eyes in the living room fixed on Katie as the message continued.

"We've seen you on TV several times now . . . and we're convinced that you're the one for us."

Katie slapped her hand down on the couch and yelled into the kitchen. "I got you a job!"

Sheila swung the refrigerator door shut and gave herself a "high-five." She straightened her collar and strutted into the living room like a peacock.

"We're in town to catch a couple of your shows,"

23

Bill continued, "and we'd like to meet with you tomorrow morning, if possible, to get acquainted and talk about the show. So . . . we'll give you a ring in the morning to set up a time and place. Until then, hope to have you on board. Ciao."

Sheila circled the room, gathering hugs and excited congratulations. She approached Julie slowly, determinedly, savoring each moment in her lover's proud gaze. No words accompanied their embrace. Julie, more than anyone, knew what this opportunity meant to Sheila. Her support was unwavering, absolute. For a moment, the two existed alone in quiet celebration.

"All right you two . . ." Sharon broke their reverie. "Dance it off at the club!"

They reluctantly ceded their embrace.

"Well then . . ." Sheila turned to the group. "I'll go put on my dancing jeans." She removed the tape from the answering machine, kissed it, and tapped Katie's belly affectionately. "Junior's gonna be rich!"

Sheila knelt before her dresser and slid open the bottom drawer. Digging beneath her sweaters from the 70s, she slowly, almost reverently, removed the cherrywood box . . . a cherished souvenir from her first trip to Provincetown with Julie. Still damp from a drizzly whale-watch, they'd wandered into an enchanting antique store. The owner, a striking woman with salt and pepper hair, had graciously fed them hot biscuits and homemade rose petal tea. The recipe seemed simple . . . boil some water, throw rose petals in . . . so Sheila brewed up a pot one night to

24

surprise Julie at the end of a candlelit anniversary dinner. Julie had taken a tentative sip, contorted her face, and got both of them laughing so hard that the tea came out her nose. Sheila knew at that moment that she would be with this woman forever.

The antique box had since been filled with a colorful array of personal keepsakes. Cards, photographs, shells, segments of "Life In Hell" torn from the Sunday paper. Sheila added the answering machine tape, her newest souvenir. She heard distant fanfare, as a bottle of champagne popped open downstairs. Probably left over from New Years Eve. Could that have been the last time they entertained . . . ?

She tried to tune out the commotion downstairs as she slid her hand back into the box and caressed the small velvet pouch. Even as she told herself not to, she watched her fingers pry it open and remove its plastic treasure. The Six Flags logo was almost entirely gone, but the photo inside looked the same when she put the tiny viewfinder to her eye.

"To my dear friend, who is certain to turn American television upside down with her irreverence." Katie lifted her Perrier in toast. The club was packed, loud, smoky. The group was congregated in a corner of the balcony, overlooking the dance floor. The steady bass rhythm pulsed through them, carrying their excitement.

"We knew you when . . . " Michelle quipped.

Sharon smirked. "And for a price, we'll keep quiet!"

"How 'bout pluggin' my concerts on your show?" Jane winked at Sheila.

Katie cleared her throat loudly. "Let's wait till the ink's dry, okay?" Partly pragmatic, partly superstitious.

"To dotted I's and crossed T's." Julie raised her glass.

"To closing the deal." Katie added hers.

Sheila tapped her tequila against the Perrier. "To closing."

"Armani suit, near the coat-check . . ." The bartender pointed.

The manager craned her neck, smiled. "She's new."

"You think?" Eliza looked again, trying to detect the usual signs: a hesitant pause just inside the door, the lighting of a cigarette, a beeline toward the back wall. But Armani strode coolly across the club, eyes scanning with polished furtiveness. Eliza shifted a few bottles down the beveled glass shelf and checked her hair in the mirror behind them. "How can you tell she's new?"

The manager stepped back into her office. "I'd remember her."

"I think it's time to go downstairs for a dance . . ." Sharon leaned past Katie and over the balcony edge.

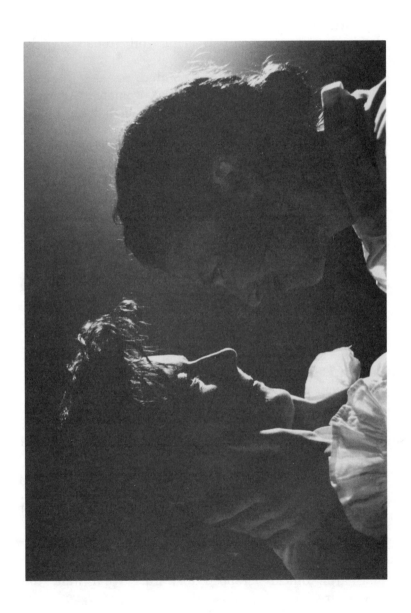

Katie chewed and swallowed an ice cube, a habit she'd acquired since swearing off tobacco. "See someone interesting?"

"Chanel suit . . ." Sharon pointed.

Michelle glanced down at the woman. "Armani," she corrected, recognizing the line which hadn't even been released yet. Well-connected woman, she thought.

Sheila refused to look, feigning outrage. "Jesus, you're only in town for one night."

"Exactly!" Sharon retorted, not missing a beat.

"And I thought you were here to see me . . ." Sheila pouted. Egging Sharon on had been a hobby since they'd first met.

"I've seen you."

Sheila turned to the group. "The loyalty of a dog in heat." She threw up her hands. The women laughed and Sheila smirked. Point. Game. Match.

"Here, here . . ." Katie interrupted the volley. "Sheila forgets what it's like to be driven by passion." She ran a hand seductively through her own thick, red hair.

"Right." Sheila put her arms around Julie from behind, pulled her close. "Now, I'm just driven by love." She spun Julie to face her. "Let's go home and work on that 'passion' thing."

Julie's slight blush was obscured by the strobing lights. "Well, practice makes perfect . . ." And it had, after all, been almost nine hours since they'd practiced.

"Goodnight ladies." Sheila beamed to the group. "It's been charming."

Sharon quickly stepped forward. "We'll walk you downstairs."

"Ah, yes." Katie linked her arm through Sharon's. "Your one night stand awaits."

"In your dreams . . ." Jane mumbled just loud enough for Sharon to hear.

Lynn set down her wine and turned, blanched, toward the woman who'd addressed her. "Excuse me?"

"I said would you like to dance?"

The woman was, by any standard, stunning. Long chocolate hair with cinnamon highlights. Speckled hazel eyes. Like the models Lynn had plastered her mirror with as a teenager. She squirmed at the recollection. "Uh . . . no, thank you."

"Okay, maybe later."

Lynn smiled halfheartedly, sipped her wine and did not look back as the woman disappeared into the lights and sound.

"She struck out!" Sharon quipped from her lookout position. "Who's up next?"

Katie poked her. "I thought you."

"She's straight." Michelle shook her head.

Katie was surprised. "You usually think everyone's gay."

"Not her." Jane chimed in.

Sharon was transfixed. "Who cares."

Katie chomped an ice cube. "So, go talk to her, Romeo."

"Romeo on the streets . . ." Sharon threw her

shoulders back. "Juliet in the sheets!" She batted her lashes.

Jane rolled her eyes and motioned toward Sharon's intended conquest. "She looks more like the damsel in distress to me."

Katie slung her arm over Sharon's shoulder. "Just remember everything you learned in therapy. You can do it."

"Right . . . like I wanna be humiliated in front of all of you?"

"Poor woman." Katie patted Sharon on the back and started toward the bar. "Where angels fear to tread . . ."

Sharon was speechless. Michelle filled the void. "Fools step in."

"I'm not here to dance," Lynn said quickly as Katie approached. Indigo eyes fixed solidly on the trespasser.

Katie stopped, still several yards away. "Oh . . . well, I'm flattered . . . but I wasn't going to ask you to dance." She glanced down at her belly.

Lynn averted her stare, grinned, looked back. "Sorry."

"That's O.K." Katie stepped up beside her and leaned against the bar. "So, why are you here?"

"I'm . . . looking for someone."

Katie knew it was nearly two a.m. The club would soon close. "Been waiting long?"

Lynn twisted the base of her wine glass and stared at the wet spirals forming on the shiny surface beneath it. "You could say that." She checked her watch, turned to Katie. "Excuse me."

Katie followed Lynn halfway to the exit, then veered off into the semi-circle of wide eyes and smiling faces. "She wants me . . . Bad!"

Jane smirked. "Obviously."

"What'd she say?" Sharon questioned zealously, eager to unwrap the tale like a gift on Christmas morning.

Katie watched the bouncer scurry to hold the door open for Lynn. "I don't think she's straight . . ."

Three heads twisted to study Lynn's departure.

The foyer was bathed in blue moonlight as Sheila turned the key and pulled Julie inside the house. Julie reached for the light switch, but Sheila intercepted her hand and put it around her own waist. "Our power bill's been far too high." She peeled back Julie's black lace top, revealing shoulders still bronze from their trip to Key West. "Have you noticed?"

Julie smiled, shook her head no.

Sheila ran her tongue along the sensitive crevice between Julie's collarbone and neck. "Well, a penny saved . . ." She pushed Julie back against the door, leaned against her. They slid along the wall and collapsed easily onto the stairs. Sheila rolled on top of Julie, felt the zippers of their jeans push together. "Why did we buy a bed?" She skated her cheek across Julie's breasts, the softest skin she'd ever felt. "We could've had a motor boat . . ." She fastened her lips gently around one nipple, then the other.

Julie pressed up against Sheila, felt her weight, folded into her. "How can you still do this to me?"

Sheila whispered, "Like this ..." and began a new journey of kisses down Julie's trembling body.

"Where have you been?" He fired the question without looking up from his Investor's Business Daily. The answer would be irrelevant but for its engagement of Lynn in an argument.

"Walking on the beach." Her tone was rehearsed, her stride past him mechanical.

"So why do your clothes smell like smoke?" Checkmate. He scanned the NASDAQ quotes.

Lynn stopped dead and flashed a cold stare. Their deluxe suite felt suddenly cramped like a cage, and she wasn't sure she'd last the whole week. At least at home she had lots of rooms to busy herself in. She stepped out onto the terrace and stared down at the marina, trying hard to lose herself in its mesmerizing sway of lights. She wondered, not for the first time, why she maintained her entanglement with this familiar stranger. But the question was too formidable to answer ... so she filed it away for another day.

Sheila studied the rise and fall of Julie's breath, watched her eyes twitch and dance in REM sleep. An image she often tried to conjure when alone in distant motel rooms. They had made love furiously, then slowly, then furiously again before drifting off to sleep. But Sheila's sleep had been brief and fitful, nightmares chasing her back into wakefulness. Always the same. Young and alone at the edge of the woods behind her childhood home. A voice calling to her from deep within the forest. She hesitates. Night is coming. The summons becomes more desperate. A few cautious steps into the mossy forest bed. Darkness rapidly closing in. A glance back toward the house which feels like goodbye. Hastening through the snarled ferns which snatch at her ankles. Voice still distant, shifting its point of origin, dodging her approach. At last an open field. Her friend romping through rows of moonlit sunflowers taller than she. They call each other's name. Race to greet. Reach to embrace. Her friend disappears. Hollow laughter echoes around her. She smells dirt and realizes she is buried.

The room felt cool as Sheila peeled the damp, twisted sheets off her body and slid out of bed. She buttoned on a nightshirt and started down the steps, almost tripping over Stella, who'd made a bed of the tangled garments abandoned there earlier. She stroked Stella back to sleep, then quietly moved into the living room.

The fireplace begged for use and Sheila obliged. A deep orange glow filled the room and sent shadows dancing up the wall. She settled cross-legged on the floor and leaned happily back against the couch she'd charmed away from her grandmother just last month — much to the dismay of her mother, who'd wanted it for years.

She noticed the stack of envelopes Katie had left

on the table. Fan mail . . . a peculiar phenomenon. For years now, baby dykes and seniors alike had graciously poured out their affection and admiration, and though she'd never gotten used to having strangers reveal themselves to her in such touching and provocative ways, it felt like a privilege and a part of her thrived on their praise.

She fanned the pile out across the glass tabletop. Judging by the return addresses, almost always neatly included, her three week tour of the northeast had been a success. There was a postcard from upstate New York, lavender stationary from Boston, something drenched in patchouli from Philadelphia . . .

And then her attention was caught by an envelope that had no address at all. Intrigued, she pulled it from the pile . . . and within moments, the handwriting delivered a blow that knocked the wind from her. Stunned and awash with unwelcome sensation, she stared . . . disconnected . . . as hands which looked like hers slowly tore through the envelope and withdrew a single page.

"I'd like to meet with you after your show. Northern Lights Cafe. L.W."

Sheila saw blackness . . . and realized her eyes were squeezed shut. She touched her face and her fingers came away wet. "Get a grip," urged a voice inside her head. She realized she wasn't breathing and forced herself to. She reread the note and noticed the logo at the top. It was from a local hotel. "Jesus Christ . . ."

Still in a daze, Sheila retrieved her jeans from the stairwell and slipped them on, inadvertently attracting the attention of Stella who, true to form, barked at the sound of jingling keys.

"Hey . . . shhh," Sheila pleaded.

Stella wagged her tail, barked again.

"Honey, what's with Stella?" A sleepy voice called from upstairs.

Sheila heaved a sigh and started climbing. She found Julie curled sweetly beneath the down comforter.

"Why is Stella barking?"

She tugged a strand of her cropped auburn hair. "She wants to go for a walk."

"Now?"

"Don't worry . . . I'll take her."

Julie wrapped the blanket around her and rolled over. "One of the many reasons I love you."

Sheila took off down the stairs without looking back.

The road was damp with cold drizzle, and Stella was displeased by the spray of passing cars on their walk to the Bayside Hotel. Sheila, dressed only in her nightshirt and jeans, was oblivious to the weather, trapped in an internal storm.

As the wind kicked up, sending the leaves into a dance that flung raindrops against her face, Sheila realized they'd been standing for a long time outside the hotel. She looked down toward the marina at the end of the road. She should probably keep walking. Sit on a dock for a while and get this out of her system. Go home and crawl into bed with Julie . . .

"Can I help you?" The desk clerk glanced disapprovingly at the wet animal in his lobby. Ever-accommodating, Stella shook herself off.

Sheila pretended to miss the exchange. "Um..." She fidgeted with some brochures on the counter. "Do you have a guest registered under the name Lynn Webster?"

The clerk typed into his computer. "I'm sorry, there's no one here by that name."

"Are you sure?"

"Positive. But there's lots of other hotels in town. Maybe..."

Sheila backed away. "Yeah... thanks anyway."

Too raw and shaken to go back to bed, Sheila continued past her front door and headed out to the beach. The long, wooden dock, with tiny white lights wrapped around its thin rails, and hand-cut planks just beginning to bear saltwater scars, had been Sheila's first addition to the house. Within days of moving in, she'd convened a group of friends for a weekend of work, music, discourse and barbecues, and by Sunday night the dock had been set afloat and christened "Wit's End."

Beneath a sliver of white that called itself the moon, Sheila climbed into her small boat and began rowing, still tied to the dock. Oars smacked and strained against the rope which held her captive... each stroke a futile exorcism of the memories flooding through her.

From the shadows of the upstairs balcony, Julie watched in silence.

Sailboat masts clanked and peaked above the gray-blue mist, celebrating the sun's morning creep across the bay. Through sleepy eyes, Julie watched the light slowly bathe the bedroom's rich blue and brown tones. The herons would soon be feeding in the water behind the house, the otters circling playfully. A phone ring pierced the calm. Julie grabbed the cord and dragged the phone across the night table. It knocked her Marlboro's to the floor, then caught on the antique silver frame, spinning the photograph slowly toward her. She and Sheila, close up, face to face, the morning after they'd first made love . . .

A pre-pregnant Katie had shown up at dawn, orange juice in one hand, champagne in the other, eager to celebrate the fall equinox. Letting herself in as always, she climbed the steps, found Sheila and Julie curled up sleeping, and crawled into bed beside them. And that was how she'd told it, when Julie rolled into her later that morning and they all woke up.

Sober enough to know for certain this woman had not been in bed with them the night before, Julie nonchalantly followed Sheila's lead and never gave it a second thought. They'd finished off the mimosas before getting out of bed, taking swigs from each container and mixing it in their mouths. The day was spent collecting driftwood and seaglass, taking photographs and discussing the relationship between desire and appetite. They ended up building a fire on the beach, laying in a pile of newly raked leaves and singing songs from Broadway musicals. Fully attuned to each other's presence and the bond forming between them, they found themselves profound and silly, awake and alive. By nightfall, a family had been born.

Julie pulled the ringing phone onto the bed. "Hello." She yawned. "No, this is Julie." She rubbed her eyes. "No, you don't have the wrong number. Hold on." She stretched toward Sheila, spoke into her ear. "Honey, it's for you."

Sheila mumbled incoherently and rolled over without opening her eyes.

"It's a man . . ." Julie extended the receiver toward her.

Sheila sprung upright. "Oh my God." She reached and covered the mouthpiece. "It must be Bill Matthews."

"Well, take it."

38

"I can't talk to him now." Sheila pulled the sheets tightly around her. "I'm naked!"

Julie chuckled. "I don't think he'll notice."

"Tell him to hold on." Sheila spotted her bathrobe hanging on the knob of her armoire. "Tell him you're my secretary."

"I think it's a bit late for that . . ."

Sheila darted from the bed.

"Um, she's on another line right now." Julie made a valiant attempt to sound serious. "Can you hold?" She buried the phone in the covers to mute her uncontrollable laughter.

Sheila knotted the belt of her terry-cloth robe, sat demurely on the edge of the bed and cleared her throat. "Hello . . . Oh, hi Bill." She rubbed her eyes. "Yeah . . . well, you know, early to bed, early to rise."

Julie smirked.

"Actually, this afternoon would be better for me. I volunteer over at the petting zoo . . ." Sheila intercepted Julie's hand, which traveled up her thigh. "I'm scheduled to be there all morning." She tightened the knot of her robe.

"Sure, that would be fine. See you then. Bye."

Sheila hung up the phone and looked at Julie. "Two o'clock."

"Early to bed and early to rise?" Julie teased.

"She's on the other line right now, please hold?" Sheila puffed an invisible cigarette.

Julie pulled Sheila down on top of her and looked her in the eye. "Here we go . . ."

A crowd of rowdy children and their parents watched with enjoyment as Sheila, muddy and disheveled, led the white donkey around the small, dirt ring. First ride went to the birthday girl, smiling with five year old aplomb in her suede cowgirl suit. Young party-goers lined the brightly-ballooned fence, vying to be next.

Sheila liked being around kids and was looking forward to her role as godmother to Katie's child. She'd already ordered a stuffed bear, "almost life-sized," from F.A.O. Schwartz, and Julie had ordered baby moccasins from L.L. Bean. Sheila knew from the moment Katie announced her pregnancy that the child would be a girl. Lucky kid, she thought, coming into the world with three mothers. Maybe she wouldn't suffer the absence of her father . . .

But Sheila knew better. Ian worked on the fishing boats that periodically set off for Alaska from Lion's Bay Port. Katie had known him since second grade, when Ian's dad, a navy officer, was transferred to the local base. Although they'd never married, they had lived together on and off for years and liked to consider themselves a couple. Katie still wasn't quite sure what had happened, but her take on it was that Ian ultimately couldn't integrate fatherhood into his self-image, and so departed the relationship in a burst of false reasons and apologies. After several months of self-recrimination, she'd finally undertaken the task of examining why she'd been involved in so casual a relationship and how she'd missed seeing this coming. Along with that process, she celebrated her entrance into the cycle of creation, and prepared to interact with a new being.

As Sheila tugged the donkey down the final stretch, she passed by Linden, a retired fireman who now ran the petting zoo almost single-handedly.

"She's worked here for years," Linden announced to the distinguished looking stranger standing beside him. "The kids really love her." He backed toward the barn, nodding proudly.

The man smiled and adjusted his bomber jacket.

Sheila shrugged modestly. "She yours?" She helped the cowgirl down from her mount.

"No . . ." The man chuckled and ran a hand through his dark curly hair. "No kids."

Sheila leaned toward him. "The kids think this is a pony." She gestured toward the ring. "Pony rides!"

As they grinned in collusion, the man was startled by a small, sandy-haired boy who tugged vigorously at his jacket.

"Hey, Mister, is it my turn to ride the donkey?"

Sheila shrugged her shoulders. "Mensa kid!"

The man lifted the boy onto the donkey's back and extended a hand to Sheila. "Bill Matthews."

"Bill . . ." Sheila reached for his hand but noticed hers was dirty. "Bill . . . Matthews . . ." She wiped it on her jeans and engaged his firm shake.

"I wanted a chance to meet you under less formal circumstances." His manner was warm, disarming.

"Can't get much less formal than this!" She pulled a patch of matted donkey hair from her sleeve.

"Better get back to work!" Bill motioned toward the donkey, who had carried the young boy off toward the peacock pen in search of grass.

Sheila dashed over and intercepted them, drawing a round of applause from amused onlookers. She watched as Bill disappeared into the crowd.

♥ ♥ ♥

Dressed only in her black cotton underwear and sportsbra, Sheila danced around the sunlit bedroom holding Stella in a tango embrace.

"Any day, you two!" Katie called from downstairs.

Julie emerged from the bathroom in a stunning charcoal gray pantsuit. "We'll be right down." She twisted a silver cufflink into place, looked Sheila up and down. "Subtle . . ."

"Well . . . you were hogging the bathroom!" Sheila shrugged.

Julie crossed toward her. "You sure you want me to go with you?"

"Definitely!" Sheila put Stella down and took Julie's hands. "It's just a hello-nice-to-meet-you type thing. I'd like to have you there."

"Well then, hurry up." Julie smacked Sheila playfully on the rear. "Unless you want to go like that . . ." She headed downstairs, gazing back over her shoulder. "Which I wouldn't mind!"

♥ ♥ ♥

Alone in the conference room, Bill had staked a place at the head of the table and spread his papers out. He flipped through a contract and spoke into his cell phone. "Section 15A is a deal-breaker, so watch it during the revisions." He heard voices in the hall and checked his watch. "I'm going into a meeting now. How soon can you get back to me?" He stood as the women filed into the room, and waved them toward a table set with coffee and pastries. "You must be kidding." Cell phone in hand, he wandered into the hall.

As Katie and Julie headed toward the food, Sheila hung back and surveyed the room. Teak furniture, brass fixtures, dark green walls lined with individually lit paintings. She wondered if she was underdressed, and felt suddenly uncomfortable in her new slacks. Had she remembered to take the tags off, or were they dangling behind her like a cruel joke? What if the tape came loose and the hems dropped? What if . . .

"So, we meet again."

She heard Bill's voice and turned around. She didn't notice he'd reached for her hand. She was singularly focused on the woman standing beside him.

Bill gestured. "My wife, uh, business partner, Lynn Matthews."

Lynn's eyes locked on Sheila. "Please forgive my delay."

Outwardly frozen and inwardly slipping into a sense of unreality, Sheila could not respond, and her silence filled the room.

Quickly drawing on her unique ability to appear insouciant, Lynn turned toward the other women. "So . . ." She stiffened as she recognized Katie from the women's club.

44

"Katie McRae." Katie offered a smile and a handshake. "Sheila's manager."

Lynn felt a slight swallow betray her relief as she gripped Katie's hand. "Nice to meet you."

Julie stepped toward her. "Julie Rosen, Sheila's partner."

"Ah..." Lynn nodded, sizing Julie up in a glance. Julie motioned toward Sheila. "And this, obviously, is Sheila."

Lynn approached Sheila and extended her hand. "Big day..."

They shared a curt handshake.

"Please excuse me..." Sheila turned and hurried out of the room.

Lynn set her briefcase on the table and smoothed her skirt. "Coffee, anyone?"

Katie backed toward the door. "I think I'll just go check on Sheila..."

Lynn forced a smile and poured her fifth coffee of the day.

Katie found Sheila in the ladies' room, doubled over beside a toilet.

"Are you okay?" She held the stall door open and looked down at her.

Sheila stared at the floor. "Katie, just go... I'll be right there."

Katie didn't move. Her mind began running through home remedies, but she wasn't sure what the problem was.

"Please..." Sheila looked up at her.

Katie had never seen her look so bad. "Sheila..."

"Please..."

Knowing Sheila would talk only when she was ready to, Katie reluctantly turned and left. She paused in the hall to recompose herself, then strode back into the conference room, smiling in a falsely casual way.

"No problem, just a touch of nerves." She crossed the room with confidence and took a seat to Bill's left, north side of the table. Her grandmother, part Tulalip Indian, had taught her to draw power from this position during negotiations. She'd only really practiced on family members, but she believed it was responsible for her parents' consent to her many entrepreneurial ventures as a child. And besides, it couldn't hurt.

"So, Sheila wants us to go ahead and she'll join us momentarily." She opened her briefcase and pulled out a notepad.

Bill leaned forward. "Well, the idea is to establish a show in which the lead character is gay, but to not have every episode dwell on that fact."

Katie smiled. "I like it already."

Sheila leaned over the sink and splashed water on her face, hoping to drown the image that pressed ceaselessly behind her eyes. Herself, twenty years old, sobbing brokenly between gasps for breath. Drenched by a downpour, curled into a ball, outside a front door. Chilling blue eyes staring from inside. Eyes she thought she'd look into forever. Eyes she thought she'd never see again.

Sheila shut off the tap and stared at her reflection in the mirror. Water dripped from her hair, marking her silk shirt with tear-like stains. She didn't really care, but she knew she was supposed to. She smoothed her hair back, then held her shirt up against the hand dryer until the warm air began to make her nauseous again.

As she approached the conference room, she could hear Bill's voice. She paused just out of view and listened.

"I must admit, I wasn't too sure about all of this at first, but Lynn was. She convinced me that the public is finally ready for something like this."

Sheila was stunned. Lynn had masterminded the whole venture . . . but why? She needed time to think, but knew she had to rejoin the meeting. As she peeked in the door, she noticed Julie looking at her. She silently mouthed "I'm okay," then stepped into the room. "Sorry," she said to no one in particular. "Please continue."

Lynn studied Sheila's quick cross of the room, and graded her "A+" for successfully avoiding any eye contact. Sheila had, clearly, developed a certain toughness over the years . . .

"I think people are ready . . ." Lynn turned to Sheila, and the pause brought Sheila's eyes to hers. "To embrace this . . . or at least accept it." She maintained her cool gaze as Sheila looked away. Beneath the table, she peeled a napkin into shreds.

Bill leaned forward, animated with enthusiasm. "We think the public is ready to sit back on those couches they love so much and give you a try!"

Lynn could detect the effort behind Sheila's weak smile, and tried to draw the attention off of her. "So . . ." She clicked open her briefcase and reached in. "We don't need to talk about details now. We've

47

drawn up some preliminary papers..." She pulled out a stack of papers and extended them toward Sheila. "Why don't you just look them over, and then we can talk more about where to go from here..."

It was a long moment before Lynn realized Sheila wasn't going to take the papers. Katie realized it too, and quickly reached for them. "We'll get right on it."

Lynn turned her attention to Katie. "We're scheduled to be here for the rest of the week, and we'd like to see a few more of Sheila's shows."

Sheila leaned forward. "A few more?"

Julie turned to Lynn. "You were there last night?"

"Well...yes." Lynn shifted in her seat and glanced unwittingly at Bill. "I mean, not really..." She looked back to Julie. "Only for a bit..."

Julie looked disappointed. "I wish we'd known. You could've sat with us."

Lynn swallowed discretely. "Well, perhaps we can plan to join you tonight?"

Katie jotted a note. "I'll put you on the list."

Lynn smiled. "I look forward to it."

Their eyes met, and they both remembered their encounter the previous night. Katie grinned slightly, while Lynn retreated behind a professional demeanor. "Well then, we'll speak further about terms and details as the week progresses."

Katie followed her lead. "I look forward to that."

Bill snapped his briefcase shut and stood. "Thank you all for your time."

Lynn sat fidgeting with contracts and paper clips as everyone made their way to the door. Bill stopped and looked at her. "Are you coming?"

She straightened a stack of paper against the

table top. "Actually, I'd like to stay and speak with Sheila for a minute. 'More informal', as you always say."

Katie put a hand on Sheila's shoulder. "No problem. We'll wait for you by the elevator."

Lynn watched the group disappear down the hall before addressing Sheila, who did not turn to face her.

"I had hoped we could meet before all this." She set the papers down. "I didn't want to catch you off guard . . ." She noticed her fingers were trembling slightly and folded her hands. "I know all of this must come as quite a surprise . . ." Sheila turned around, glaring. "The offer is real, Sheila."

Sheila's eyes narrowed. She leaned forward and spoke in a measured tone. "Beware the stranger bearing gifts."

Lynn recognized this posture. Sheila was preparing to retreat. "I wanted to talk to you . . ." She attempted to delay her. "I'm ready . . . and . . . I hoped this would be a good way to get your attention."

"Interesting strategy, but I'm about fifteen years past talking." Sheila turned sharply and walked out the door.

Lynn fixed her eyes on the floor and mounted a body-wide effort to hold back her tears.

Sheila watched her reflection disappear as the brass doors of the elevator slid open. She entered and stood against the back wall, wishing she could disappear herself. She stiffened as Julie slid an arm around her.

Katie hurried in behind them, grinning like the cat that ate the canary. "You guys are not gonna

51

believe this." She pushed the "close door" button incessantly. "Mizz Lynn Matthews was at the club last night, looking for someone..."

Sheila felt herself sinking faster than the elevator, but donned a look of indifference.

Julie eagerly took the bait. "How do you know she was looking for someone?"

"I talked to her." Katie smiled, self-impressed. "I think she's straddling both sides of the fence."

Sheila stared up at the floor numbers and tried to pretend she was somewhere else.

"What?" Julie's tone was incredulous. "You think she's gay?"

Katie shrugged her shoulders. "Well, the queen of gay radar should know..." She nudged Sheila playfully. "What do you think?"

Sheila kept her eyes on the numbers. "She's not gay."

"Well then," Katie taunted, "what was she doing in the club?"

Sheila felt claustrophobic.

"Well you were in the club." Julie smirked. "And unless I'm completely out of the loop..." She leaned forward and whispered, "You're not gay."

"Touché!"

The elevator doors slid open and Sheila bolted out. Katie lagged behind Julie, still musing. "I wonder what her husband thinks..."

The evening breeze set the chimes ringing and crossed into the bedroom through the terrace door. Sheila felt her linen shirt sticking to her freshly showered skin. Framed in the cherrywood mirror, she could see that it lay asymmetrical, improperly fastened. She yanked at the collar, popping a button onto the floor. "Shit!"

"What's with you today?" Julie's voice came from behind her.

She spun around and tugged at her shirt. "It's just these fucking buttons!"

Julie shook her head. "I don't think so . . ."

"Oh really?" She bent and half-heartedly searched the floor. "What do you think?"

"I think my girlfriend has disappeared and a troll has taken over her body!"

She stood and returned Julie's smile, despite herself. "Sorry . . ."

Julie spotted the button beneath the armoire and handed it to Sheila.

"Thanks." She pulled Julie into a hug. "What would I do without you?"

Julie took a step back and looked at her. "Walk around with your shirt half-open."

She looked down at her shirt. "How to make friends and . . ." When she looked up, Julie was gone. "Influence people."

She turned and studied her reflection in the mirror. Lines under the eyes added character, right? And those six lightning bolt strands of gray hair darting through her auburn crop . . . merely a tribute to how far she'd come. And she could always pull them out if she went too far.

"Relationships . . ." Centered in a cone of white

spotlight, Sheila faced a sold-out room. "That's it, basically... that's the joke." She rubbed her chin pensively. "You know, I think it's a helluva lot easier to be straight than gay..." She awaited the protest and received it with a smile. "Listen... hear me out... Straight relationships have, you know, rules. There's a structure to them. You date, have sex... move in together, have more sex... get married, have... kids... Maybe have sex real quiet-like on Saturday morning while the kids are in front of the cartoons... Whoopie!"

She spun in a circle, then recomposed herself. "Lesbians, on the other hand, we have the sequence right... but our timing's off. We'll meet somebody, maybe someone's fixed us up, you know... our ex-lover's new ex-lover who she wants to pawn off on us now..." Chuckles of recognition spread through the crowd. "Anyway, we go out on a date... pull apart a few lobsters and do that nonchalant lick the butter off your fingers thing... Then after dinner, we drive around the suburbs looking for 'For Sale' signs."

She extended her arm and steered an invisible wheel. "Look, Honey..." She pointed to her right. "There's one with a yard big enough to host the softball barbecue." She swung an invisible bat and watched an invisible ball soar into the crowd. "Once we know the size of the house we'll be moving into, we go directly to the Humane Society to adopt the appropriate number of cats..." She folded her arms as if cradling a baby, and pleaded with her imaginary date. "Yes I know I already have four... I clean their litter boxes, you think I don't know that? But

this one has six toes. Look how cute she is! None of mine have six toes..."

"She has four cats?" The blue and red club lights cast a combination of purple and shadow across Bill's face, highlighting his strong features.

"No, no." Katie chuckled, noticing for the first time that Bill was handsome. "Just Stella."

Lynn leaned across the small, marble table. The candlelight set her eyes sparkling. "Stella?"

"Short dog, long nose." Katie gestured for emphasis. "Of course, we're not allowed to say that in front of Stella... Sheila says it hurts her feelings."

Lynn did not hear the story Katie went on to tell. She was lost in time. Seventeen years old... in the guest house that sat at the back of her parent's property... curled under a blanket on the couch... legs tangled with Sheila's...

The Friday night ritual would start with Sheila's arrival for dinner, during which they'd speak in code and find themselves hilarious. With a kiss on the cheek to each parent, they'd excuse themselves early and move upstairs. By 11:30, Father would be shuffling through papers in his study, Mother propped up in bed watching Johnny Carson to see what the women were wearing. Sheila would go first — out Lynn's bedroom window, down the trellis, onto the pool deck. She always went first, so she could watch Lynn climb down. It amused her to see Lynn in compromising positions, and she cultivated opportunities to do so. Lynn knew this. She also knew they could easily have slipped out the front door but, for some reason, never suggested it.

Settled in at the guest house, they'd build a fire

and make Jiffy Pop. Sometimes they'd concoct drinks from the stocked bar. On rare occasions, Sheila would bring a joint handed down from her older brother. And at 12:00 PM, without fail, they'd be on the couch in front of the TV singing along with the "Midnight Madness" theme song. The show featured B-grade horror movies, and was hosted by a woman in a gothic looking black gown and elbow length black sequined gloves — Stella. Stella told bad jokes and made fun of the films. She was the best part of the show, and had become somewhat of a local cult figure. Sheila and Lynn would argue each week over who was going to have a daughter first and name her Stella. For a while, they'd even taken to calling each other by that name . . .

Lynn swallowed half her glass of wine and tried to come up with other reasons Sheila's dog might be named Stella. She couldn't think of a single one.

"So, where was I?" Sheila pretended to straighten the tie painted on the front of her shirt. "Oh yeah, the date . . . We FINALLY go home and have great sex . . . for the last time . . ." She approached a woman in the front who was laughing particularly loudly. "Been there? Done that?" The woman slid down in her seat and Sheila winked at her. "The next morning, after *lattes,* we're out renting U-Hauls. Ah, the love life of a lesbian." She skipped around in a circle, singing. "Too much for me, too much for me, mortgage rates are down . . ."

Sheila paced the stage. Should she mention the TV show, or would that jinx it? She reached for the glass of water which always sat on the stool to her right. Great stall tactic. She sipped slowly and remembered quickly that the show was already jinxed.

57

"So, now that we're all inti . . . inti . . ." She cleared her throat. "Intimate . . ." She trembled at the word in her trademark fashion. "You all can be the first to know that I have a shot at my own TV show."

Enthusiastic cheers spread through the crowd.

"Thanks! And the producers are here tonight . . . so laugh like hell!"

Katie smiled at Bill, who leaned toward Lynn and spoke under his breath. "One of them was here LAST night."

"Don't start with that again." Lynn shifted her chair away from him while smiling casually at Katie.

It was difficult for Sheila to see into the audience with the stagelights beaming down on her. Columns of colored cigarette smoke spiraled toward the ceiling, conspiring to obscure her view. But, while scanning the crowd to point out "the producers," she inadvertently witnessed the exchange between Lynn and Bill. The body language was unmistakable, and for a moment she felt a guilty pleasure. Then, she noticed Julie's absence at the table . . .

The sudden glare of a spotlight shifting onto her face reminded Sheila she was on stage. She unbuttoned her top button and squeezed the back of her neck. "So we've talked about the dating thing . . . Let's talk about the bar scene for a moment, shall we? I learned all about it at dyke training school." She approached a straight couple in the front row. "Did you know we have schools now?" The man smiled and shook his head. The woman stared down at her lap, frantically twisting her Rolex round and round her wrist.

Sensing the woman's discomfort, Sheila focused her attention on the man. "Yeah, we're franchising, Sir . . . Really branching out." She squared her hands to form a marquee. "Dorothy's School for Baby Dykes: you don't know what you've been missing." The man laughed heartily and the woman glared at him. Sheila knew the type. This woman would undoubtedly repeat Sheila's jokes at the next cocktail party but run rings around herself to avoid saying the word "dyke."

"Don't I know you from there, Ma'am?" Sheila couldn't resist. "Class of '79?"

The woman looked to her husband, who made a chivalrous but failed attempt not to laugh along with the crowd.

"Case of mistaken identity, perhaps . . ." Sheila shrugged her shoulders innocently. "We all look alike, you know." She winked at the man — who, unbeknownst to her, silently ran through fuzzy half-memories of locker room encounters he'd never managed to categorize.

"My favorite class was bar etiquette, where we learned how to choose a suitable wall, stand in groups, smoke a lot, and whisper like the Olympics rating committee." She flipped imaginary scorecards and tracked passing beauties with her eyes. "Six point four . . . five point nine . . . eight point one . . . German judge, two . . ." She pretended to light a cigarette and take a drag. "Your mission, should you choose to accept it: find the woman with the most cat hair on her clothes. Meet her. Marry her." She squashed the cigarette under her boot. "Simple class. Got an 'A.' "

Things, of course, were never really that simple. And maybe she shouldn't perpetuate the myth of easy, uncomplicated love. But it always got a laugh.

"Straight women, on the other hand ... What they're looking for, if you can believe what you read in 'New Woman,' is that special someone who doesn't spend the whole night watching sports on the bar TV, great clothes, good dancer, nice tight butt..." She feigned contemplation, then surprise. "Oh my God... I think I'm straight!" She rubbed her chin. "Which means my personal ad is running in the wrong section of the paper ... Maybe you've seen it. 'GWF, 35 ...' "

"Seen it!" hailed a voice from her left.

Sheila turned and spotted the offender, a young bartender she recognized from the club. "And you didn't call? How could you resist?" She cocked her head and grinned through the applause.

Eliza smiled and leaned back in her chair, knowing full well that Sheila was a happily married woman. The lesbian community routinely telegraphed such information, and Sheila's metamorphosis had generated intense discussion and speculation over dinner tables and pool tables alike. Eliza had even considered using the topic as a conversation starter last night with the Armani goddess, but the woman's hasty departure had nipped her romantic aspirations in the bud ...

"For those of you who missed it," Sheila continued reciting her personal ad, " 'GWF, 35, aloof, internal, unable to commit. Sarcastic. Given to bouts of infantilism. Can burp the alphabet . . .' " That always drew a round of applause, and her closest friends knew it was true. " 'Seeking caretaking-earthmother with no boundaries, for travel through inner space in search of perfect union. Healthy people need not apply.' "

The gallery was dark, except for a slash of light that escaped the back office and pierced the room. Julie leaned up against a file cabinet and checked her watch. It had been a long evening, spent organizing receipts and miscellaneous paperwork. Though she found this aspect of her work less gratifying than the creativity that spawned it, she had a natural savvy for business and considered it a welcome burden of success.

She thought she heard knocking coming from the front of the gallery, and flipped on the main lights. A familiar silhouette stood outside the front window, eerily illuminated by the flickering, amber streetlight. As she crossed the room, Sheila pressed her head up against the glass and stared at her.

Julie unlocked the door and swung it open. "How'd the show go?"

Sheila brushed past her. "You would know if you'd been there."

Julie silently counted to ten. "I thought you needed some space." She smiled.

Sheila took Julie's arms and put them around her back. "This is the space I want."

For a moment they stood in quiet embrace, and Julie could feel Sheila's heart beating against her. "Lots of excitement, huh?"

"Lots." Sheila broke from the embrace and began roaming through the gallery.

"Did they come to the show?"

Sheila fixed her eyes on a painting. "Who?"

"Who . . . ?" Julie stepped in front of her.

"Oh . . . yeah." Sheila dodged Julie and circled a blown glass display. "They were there."

Julie followed close behind. "Were you nervous? What did they think? Did they like you?"

"I don't know." Sheila stopped. "We didn't actually talk." She held a cobalt vase up to the light and looked through it. "You should paint the gallery purple."

Feeling a tinge of frustration, Julie pushed aside a basket of business cards and sat on the edge of her antique desk. "Sometimes I don't get you."

"Yeah, me neither. It's just . . . everything's a bit much right now." Sheila set the vase down and turned to Julie. "Okay?"

Julie reminded herself that any type of change, good or bad, always seemed a struggle for Sheila. And though she knew it wasn't her responsibility to make Sheila feel better, she could at least try not to make her feel worse. She hopped down from the desk and took Sheila's hand. "Okay."

Sheila lifted Julie's hand to her lips and kissed it. "This troll's ready to go home."

Go play outside!" Katie admonished Duchess, a black standard poodle, who did not budge but instead stared up at Katie with the same willful eyes Stella used on Sheila. Katie was glad Sheila was in the living room, unable to bear witness as she took hold of Duchess' green bandanna and coaxed her slowly down the back steps.

The sun warmed Katie's face and threw golden highlights into her wavy, red hair. Mother nature had provided another amazing spring day. Katie thanked the four directions, as her grandmother had taught her, and inhaled the breeze which swept down from Lion's Head Mountain. Sage . . . and lavender. Ian used to hike in the mountains and return home with pockets full of lavender . . .

She headed back into the house, setting fire under a kettle as she passed through the kitchen. Rounding the corner into the living room, she found Sheila exactly as she'd left her; perched on the edge of the couch, wiping a coffee-soaked napkin across the glass table. Duchess had tumbled Sheila's cherished "joy tonic" while in pursuit of Shag, the newly adopted guinea pig. Katie had found the spectacle funnier than Sheila, and tried to hide her grin. "Sorry about that."

Sheila swiped at a coffee stream escaping toward the edge of the table. "It shifted shape like mercury, and snaked into brown rivulets . . . carrying tiny napkin-shred canoes to certain demise in the oriental rug below."

"Huh?"

Sheila lifted a stack of paper from the table and began carefully peeling apart the wet pages. "It's an omen."

"A good one!" Katie settled into her red leather chair, which was well-worn and easily accommodated her extra thirty-two pounds. "Mirage seems to have figured everything out to the last detail." She examined several pages laid out on the table. "Hardly preliminary. All that's left to do is sign on the dotted line . . ."

"Or not."

"Why do they call it a dotted line?" Katie gestured toward the papers. "It's never dotted . . . it's always just a regular straight line." She looked up as Sheila's comment finally registered. "Or not?"

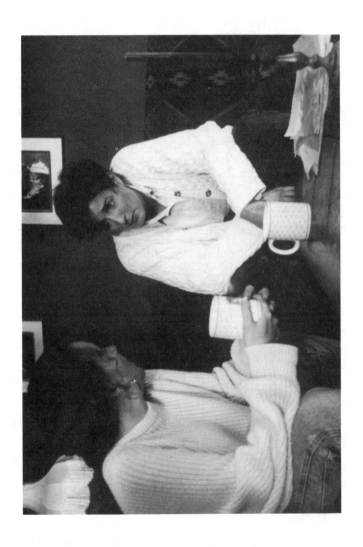

Sheila leaned forward. "Well, it IS a business decision. I need to think about it."

Katie sipped her coffee and studied Sheila. "What's to think about?"

"All this!" Sheila waved her arm over the papers. "It's all their terms. What about my terms?" As soon as the words came out she regretted them. They sounded defensive. She needed to sound . . . regular. But then again, maybe being defensive was regular for her. Her therapist seemed to think so. Jan had diagnosed her as an inveterate intellectualizer, with tendencies toward humor. "Two high-level defense mechanisms," Sheila often quoted proudly. "Even found a way to make money off them," she'd tell herself and others . . . knowing that such telling was, itself, intellectualization and humor. But she fiercely romanced these twin muses, sensing that if they ever refused to perform, she would be left alone with the scary prospect of her self.

Accustomed to Sheila's "histrionic moments," an undistracted Katie spread several contract pages across her knees. "The money looks good. The schedule looks good. The exposure would be un-believable." She looked up at Sheila. "Exactly what terms are you unhappy with?"

Sheila shrugged. "It's just . . . too fast. Not what I expected."

Katie leaned back and rubbed her belly. "Surprises like this you can live with!"

Julie's wrists pivoted with precision — slashing, sloping, skating — pulling the charcoal stick along in

a dance across the page. She felt passion-filled, surrounded by her favorite things. Fresh, wet clay piled by the door, sandpaper dust floating through cones of sunlight, paints radiating their color-coordinated scents. She inhaled deeply and smiled. "Vermilion."

She'd been able to smell color since childhood, and didn't realize most people couldn't until the afternoon Mom sat her up on the kitchen table for a talk. Though the explanation was nebulous at best, Julie got the gist. "It's fine to know so, but not to say so." Still at an age of holding up fingers to show how old she was, she wondered why but didn't ask. At thirty-three, she still didn't really understand. She knew her mother must have been right, because "saying so" had always led to ridicule in the intervening years. But when, in a moment of forgetfulness, she'd told Sheila that her favorite smell was chartreuse, Sheila had simply smiled and replied, "I think mine's burnt sienna." Burnt sienna . . . The most romantic words she'd ever heard.

She took a step back and surveyed her work. The sketch was coming along quickly. The design seemed to be evolving of its own accord. She turned up the Indigo Girls and sang along in an "I-can't-hear-anything-I'm-wearing-headphones" tone of voice.

Sheila could hear Julie's dulcet tones as she approached the house. She went directly upstairs and poked her head into the studio, just in time to catch an impressive pirouette. "Performance art?"

Julie pulled off her headphones, startled. "Hey . . ." She grabbed a paint-stained sheet from the floor and threw it over the drawing.

Sheila grinned. "Work in progress?"

"It's a surprise . . ."

Sheila stepped into the room and approached the easel. "For who?"

"Gee . . ." Julie put her hands on Sheila's shoulders and forced her backward toward the door. "One can only imagine!"

Sheila bent forward and kissed her.

"Forget it." Julie tried to sound stern . . . a difficult air to maintain as Sheila's hands crept into her overalls and slid under her tank top.

"Are you sure?" Sheila felt Julie's nipple harden. "I could stay . . . and see it." She ran her tongue along the sensitive nape of Julie's neck.

For a moment, Julie considered maneuvering Sheila onto the drafting table and making love to her. But she knew it would become an all-day event, and she needed to get some work done. "Off with you, temptress!" She gave Sheila a quick kiss and pointed her toward the door.

Sheila twisted open a bottle of ouzo, hand-carried back from last year's pilgrimage to Santorini. She lined up three shot glasses and splashed some into each. Reggae music and the smell of paella drifted through the house. Guests filled the living room and spilled out onto the back deck. Familiar faces, collected over the years. New friends and old lovers. She sauntered through the crowd, brushing gently against Julie as they crossed paths at the sliding glass door. Brass lanterns cast a golden glow on the deck, highlighting the marble and malachite sculptured pieces which lined its periphery. Sheila danced over and handed drinks to Michael and Angelique. "Your cocktails..." She raised her own glass in a toast.

Angelique loosened her scarf and smiled. "You're in good spirits tonight!"

Sheila reclined into her favorite beach chair and looked out at the bay, whose rolling crests sparkled dark-purple in the moonlight. "Just happy to be home for more than two days."

"Socializing with the common folk," Michael teased.

She leaned forward and squeezed his knee. "Yeah, right." He motioned toward the house. She turned and saw Julie dancing in the living room, making wings of her skirt as she swayed soulfully. "That woman recaptures my heart every day."

"I think she's glad you're here," Angelique commented.

"Why?" Sheila turned to her. "Did she say something?" She felt a momentary pang of guilt about her constant travel, though Julie had never made an issue of it. At least not with her.

Michael leaned forward, eyebrows raised.

"Company!" Angelique pointed toward the yard.

"We rang the bell..."

Sheila turned and saw Lynn standing behind her.

"Nobody answered..." Lynn shifted left and right, twisted her Movado timepiece. Bill came up beside her and nodded hello to the group.

Julie spotted the couple and dashed out onto the deck. "Great! You decided to come!" She took Bill by the hand. "Come on in, I'll introduce you around." She tugged him into the house.

Sheila stood and faced Lynn. "For fifteen years

you're nowhere..." she spoke in measured tones, "and now every time I turn around, you're in my face!"

Lynn made a half-hearted attempt not to smile. "Or maybe, I accidentally put on my contacts that have YOU painted on the inside."

They shared a lengthy and unflinching gaze — until Lynn freed a full and devastating smile.

"I hate when you do that..." Sheila felt fifteen years of defenses melting in the pit of her belly.

"Are you guys gonna stand there all night or what?" Julie called as she came around the corner.

Sheila looked away. She caught the moon ducking behind a thin cloud, and wished she could join it.

Lynn tightened the band around her hair. "Bathroom...?"

Julie pointed. "Upstairs, down the hall, on the right." She watched Lynn disappear into the crowd. "I like her."

Sheila felt a sudden need to hold Julie close. She put her arms around her from behind. "I like you." The feeling that she was trying to convince herself of something was, thankfully, fleeting.

Lynn slowly climbed the stairs into a darkened room. An antique candelabra was centrally hung, providing the only light. Wooden beams threw dark, angular shadows against the indigo walls. As her eyes adjusted, she could make out a brick fireplace, an Ikea futon-couch, a Pier One wicker chair. A terrace ran the length of the room, fronting the bay.

Lynn stepped outside and inhaled the moist night

air. Across the water, tiny lights ran up the mountainside, becoming increasingly isolated with height. She could hear Sheila's voice from the deck below. Her laugh . . .

The wind seemed to pick up suddenly, and she stepped back inside. But her chill was quickly replaced by the burning sensation which spread through her chest as, for the first time, she spotted a bed against the opposite wall and realized where she was. She looked around the room with new eyes. Eyes that wanted to see and not see in equal measure. What they saw was bold, colorful paintings, marked with Julie's signature. Framed photographs from parties and vacations. Shelves full of favorite books and video tapes. A small dog . . . Stella . . . asleep near the couch. Lynn's eyes saw a life. A life which bore no mark of her. Had she expected something different?

She crossed the room and sat on the edge of the bed. Beside her, she noticed a silver picture frame on the nightstand. She lifted it for a closer look, angled it toward the light. Julie and Sheila . . . close up, in profile . . . sharing a look she'd seen on other faces, but never her own.

"Bathroom?"

Lynn looked up, startled to find a woman standing by the top of the steps. "I . . . was looking for it myself."

The woman's eyes swept slowly across the room. "Many have visited . . ." She smiled. "But only one's been invited to stay."

Lynn stood and replaced the photograph on the nightstand. "Romantic . . ."

The woman shook her head with a curious

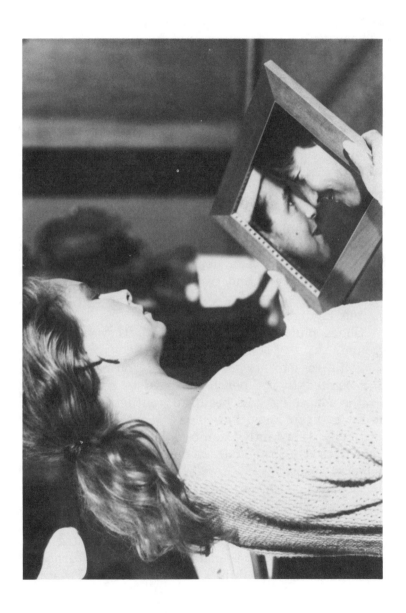

knowing. Lynn maneuvered around her and retreated downstairs.

"Well, okay..." Sheila leaned back in her chair, lifting its front legs off the ground. "But I still think bisexuals are greedy."

"Face it, Bill..." Julie feigned seriousness. "You're just another lesbian trapped in a man's body." She leaned across Katie and poked Bill in the leg.

"Well, thanks..." He shrugged. "I guess..."

Sheila spotted Lynn making her way toward them. She dropped her chair forward. Exit stage left, she thought. She stood and gestured toward her chair.

"No, that's okay..." Lynn looked around. "I'll sit on the ground."

Sheila blurted a laugh. "Lynn Matthews sit on the ground?"

Katie rose to her feet. "No, no! You can sit here." She pointed to the bench. "I have to go mingle and do the charming and beautiful routine." She winked at Lynn. "You know how it is."

Sheila reluctantly slumped back into her chair. Lynn forced a grin and sat down beside Julie. "Your home is lovely."

"Thanks. I mean, it's Sheila's house..." Julie turned to Sheila. "But I've been here so long it feels like my house too."

"It is your house." Sheila punctuated the statement with a quick glare at Lynn, then turned to Bill. "The artwork's Julie's. Most of her stuff's at her gallery, downtown. You should check it out while you're here."

Julie felt awkward about the plug, but Bill seemed genuinely impressed. "Maybe we could use some of your pieces in the show."

"Why not!" Julie joked. "Nepotism is relative!"

Bill stalled, trying to download the definition of nepotism from his memory. "So . . ." He lit a cigarette. "How long have you two been . . . 'relatives?' "

"Four and a half years." Julie looked at Sheila. "Not including those first few months where all you do is stay in bed . . . eat Chinese food . . ." Her voice trailed off.

"Chopsticks or forks?" Lynn quipped, hoping to gloss over the mention of bed.

"Fingers . . ." Julie turned to Lynn. "Mostly." She pulled a pack of cigarettes from her denim jacket.

Bill chuckled. He respected strong women, and this one could certainly fend for herself. He offered her a light.

"Nice lighter." She dangled her cigarette into the flame.

"Anniversary present." He smiled proudly.

"How long?"

Bill reached and put a hand on Lynn's knee. "Fourteen years."

Sheila shook her head. "Unbelievable . . ."

Lynn shifted position, finessing a disengagement.

"No kidding!" Julie concurred.

A glass shattered in the house, followed by a frantic call. "Hey, Sheila, where's the broom?"

Sheila jumped to her feet. "The life of a hostess!"

"I'll get it." Julie stood.

"No, I'll get it." Sheila was firm. "You stay and entertain our guests."

"That's okay." Lynn stood. "We should leave. I have work to do."

Bill seemed surprised. "Work?" He rose from his chair and looked out at the water. "How can you even think about work?"

Julie tugged at his sleeve. "Come check out the view." She escorted him toward the dock.

Although they were alone on the deck, Sheila spoke to Lynn in a whisper. "Fourteen years?" Her voice was filled with contempt. "Quick turnaround."

Lynn watched Sheila vanish into the living room. Same old Sheila, she thought. Exit, stage left.

"Hey, Lynn . . ." Julie waved from the water's edge.

Lynn climbed down from the deck and crossed the sand. The air was cooler by the water. It felt good.

"We go dancing at Celebrities most nights, if you ever want to join us." Julie ran a hand through her windblown curls and looked at Lynn. "It's that women's club . . ."

Lynn's heart thudded with alarm. She looked away.

Julie stalled. "It's down on the main street . . ." She bent and picked up a piece of driftwood. "You can't miss it." She playfully poked Bill with the branch. "It's cross-cultural, so you can come too."

Bill held up his hands and smiled. "I think I'll pass."

A voice called from the deck. "Anyone ready to go to the club?"

"Count me in!" Julie yelled back.

"Thank you for having us." Lynn shook Julie's hand.

"Well, I hope it's only the first time." Bill smiled and zipped his jacket. "I trust it is."

Sheila pulled the broom mindlessly across the linoleum, dragging glass shards from pile to pile. She could feel herself aging . . . she'd be old before this ordeal was done. Lynn had returned to suck the life out of her, what little she hadn't already stolen. To drain her vitality like a lusty vampire with an unquenchable thirst . . .

She turned on the tap and splashed her face with water. Her mind spun with an ancient craziness, frightening and all too familiar.

Julie grabbed her from behind. "Let's go to the club and get wild on the dance floor!" She spun Sheila around in a deranged salsa.

Sheila leaned back against the counter and tried to regroup. "I'm not really up for it." She turned and shut off the tap.

Katie poked her head into the kitchen. "Are you ladies ready?"

"I guess I'm flying solo tonight." Julie pouted.

Katie looked at Sheila. "You're not coming with us?"

"No, I think I'll just stay home . . ." She searched for a punchline. "And masturbate!" Lame . . . way lame, but she was in a pinch.

"Party pooper!" Julie half-joked.

"C'mon, let's go." Katie linked her arm through

77

Julie's. "That way she has to clean up!" They aimed a mutual "so there" look at Sheila, and disappeared into the foyer.

"Keep those women away from her, Katie!" Sheila maintained her jocular facade until the door closed behind them. And then she could fend off her plummet no longer.

Bill propped up a pillow and laid back on the bed. He watched Lynn gather her travel iron, steamer and spray starch. He knew she would set up on the dining table and spend the next half hour or so pressing all the clothes she'd worn that day — and he watched the news while she did just that. As she hung her final shirt in the closet, he shut off the television.

Lynn caught her reflection in the mirrored closet door. A new line had wedged itself under her left eye. A memo, of sorts, reminding her to replenish her Fountain Of Youth Face Emollient supply. Nivea should serve well enough for tonight, she convinced herself, rubbing her cheeks with it in the gentle, clockwise motion specified on the jar.

Bill folded back the blanket on Lynn's side of the bed as she reentered the room. But Lynn picked up her briefcase from the desk and settled into the other bed. She spread the sit-com contract across her lap, slipped on her reading glasses.

Bill grabbed the remote control off the nightstand, punched "On," and raised the volume just loud enough to make his presence felt.

♥ ♥ ♥

Sheila braced herself against the sink as her downward spiral began. She felt herself swirling like water sucked down a drain. And then the blitz of images came. Rain, spilling from the roof, spraying into the house through an open door. Lynn, young and far too beautiful, waving wildly, screaming. Herself, stepping backwards, pelted by wet needles. A lock spins shut. She pounds the door, collapses to the ground, cries harder than the rain.

"You're still up..." Julie's voice jarred her back into the present.

"Huh?" She found herself hunched over the sink. She felt numb and not fully present.

"You should've come." Julie opened the refrigerator and stared in. "The club was packed!"

Sheila realized the tap was running full-force into an already overflowing sink. She shut it off and wiped the counter, acting casual. "Any interesting women?"

"Hundreds." Julie popped open a soda. "Actually..." She took a gulp and smiled coyly. "All the interesting women stayed home tonight."

Sheila hung the dishtowel over the faucet and turned to Julie. "Flattery will get you everywhere..."

Julie put her drink down on the counter. She slipped off her vest and unbuttoned her collar. "I wish you would've told me that last night." She swung the vest over her shoulder, pivoted and dashed upstairs.

Sheila recognized the invitation to pursue, but could not accept it. Struggling under the weight of Lynn, Julie's touch would be unbearable.

Lynn stepped out of the taxi, straight into an ankle-deep puddle. It had been raining since sunrise. She knew this because she'd awakened from a dream at four-thirty AM, and had been unable to fall back to sleep. She'd sat on the balcony for hours watching tugboats pulling tankers, herons dive-bombing fish, seaplanes shuttling travelers. Everything seemed in motion and full of purpose.

She closed her umbrella, shook it, and slid it into the brass rack by the door. The gallery had an echo to it, and she could hear Julie speaking with a customer. She moved along the wall and studied her from a distance. Julie was animated and effusive, in mid-explanation of some new technique she'd learned for casting with fiberglass. She seemed entirely professional, yet at the same time, relaxed and gregarious. Lynn was impressed, perhaps slightly envious.

She wandered through the room, examining the diverse works of art — lithographs, stained glass, ceremonial masks. She mentally tested each piece to determine where it might fit in her house. For her, acquiring artwork was more a skill than a passion. Her purchasing power allowed her to surround herself with beautiful creations, but she was always left feeling somehow inferior to the creators themselves. She could make the argument that producing television programs was a creative act, but she never fully convinced herself.

"Lynn . . ." Julie stepped from behind a pottery display. "How are you?" She caught a whiff of Lynn's perfume and wondered what it was. Something unpronounceable, no doubt.

"I'm fine, thank you." Lynn glanced at Julie, then turned back toward the wall. "Your work really appeals to me."

"Thanks."

Lynn crossed to the pottery. "By the way . . ." She lifted a vase and studied it. "Thanks again for inviting us to the party. It was really . . . interesting." She exchanged the vase for a bowl.

"Interesting?" Julie chuckled. "Well, you should've come to the club with us!"

"The club" was not a topic Lynn wanted to

discuss. "Oh, well, I have a great deal of work to do . . . with the show and other projects, you know . . . so I don't really get out much."

A customer called from the register. "Excuse me, Miss."

Julie nodded and leaned toward Lynn. "Don't you hate that 'Miss' business?"

Lynn would never admit she hadn't thought about it. She busied herself looking at some jewelry, while Julie sprinted off to make a sale. She saw a ring she liked, and a brooch, then noticed a sculpture on a pedestal nearby. A woman's body, from torso to thighs — reminiscent of the Greek sculptures she'd studied in art history, back when she'd aspired toward museum curatorship. She lifted the piece carefully by its base, finding it surprisingly heavy for its eighteen-or-so inches. It was smooth, precise, white as Aspen's ski slopes. It strangely moved and intrigued her. "I really like this," she heard herself say aloud.

Julie looked over from the desk. "It's one of my favorites." She handed the customer his package and joined Lynn by the pedestal. "It's Sheila."

Lynn set the piece down and quickly retracted her hands. Seeking distraction, she returned to the jewelry case. "I think I'll take these two." She pointed.

Julie opened the case and removed the silver ring and pearl brooch. "Exquisite taste!" She carried them to the desk and began wrapping.

Lynn randomly locked her eyes on a nearby bird cage. Her heart was pounding. "And the sculpture."

"The sculpture?" Julie looked up. "It's twelve hundred dollars..."

"No problem." She felt in her own territory at last. "As long as you accept traveler's checks."

"Honey..." Julie leaned forward on the desk. "I take plastic, greenbacks, Deutsche marks, yen, baseball cards, and stamps!" She grinned. "And, of course, traveler's checks!"

Lynn approached the desk and pulled out her wallet. "Perfect."

Julie watched Lynn sign her way through a stack of checks, using a pen that was a piece of art itself — gold, inlaid with bands of malachite and onyx, and initialed "L.W."

Maiden name, perhaps? Julie wondered, as she crossed the room to retrieve the sculpture. She really didn't know much about this woman who was swiftly rising to prominence in her life. She stood by the pedestal and looked back at Lynn. "This isn't going to be something you just use to accentuate your furniture, is it?"

Lynn turned and smiled. "Not a chance." She watched as Julie lifted the sculpture and brought it to the desk. "Sheila comes down from her pedestal."

Julie chuckled. "Don't tell her that!" She boxed the sculpture with the jewelry and handed it to Lynn. "All yours." She felt a strange sensation as Lynn took the package from her hands, but then again, it was always hard to let go of the pieces Sheila modeled for.

Lynn pushed the checks across the desk. "Thank you."

"No, thank you!" Julie watched as Lynn breezed out the door. She fanned the traveler's checks like playing cards and smiled. "Dinner for two at the Seven Seas . . ."

♥ ♥ ♥

"Isn't the government wonderful in its approach to gay people?" Sheila pulled a small newspaper clipping from inside her jacket and paced the stage. "A friend cut this out of the paper for me. If you have a low insanity threshold, this is going to send you over the edge." She waved the clipping at the audience. "Here is where our tax dollars are being spent. This brought a lot up for me." She tried to sound serious. "It's about sheep sex . . ."

Sheila held up the clipping. "Anne Perkins, a University of California grad student, on her study of the sexuality of sheep . . ." She began to read. " 'It is very difficult to look at the possibility of lesbian sheep, because if you are a female sheep, what you do to solicit sex is to stand still. Maybe there is a female sheep out there really *wanting* another female, but there is just no way for us to know it . . .' "

Sheila tossed the clipping into the air. "I don't know, sounds like women's night to me!" She stood wide-eyed and motionless. "That oh-so-sought-after doe in the headlights look."

Katie twisted a lemon into her cranberry juice. "She's in rare form tonight."

Julie cocked her head, smiled. "That's my girl!"

Sheila lifted both hands into the air. "Okay, Ladies and Gentlemen!" She spoke like a televange-list. "The time is now . . . to open up your wallets and

lay out those big bucks for a worthy cause. As you probably know, the proceeds from tonight's show are being donated to PFLAG, which is the Parents and Friends of Lesbians and Gays, and also to CALM, the Community Alliance for Lesbian Mothers." Applause rippled through the audience. "So let's get down to some serious business. I am donating myself to this worthy cause."

"You mean DEDICATING!" A young man heckled from the side of the room.

Sheila turned in the man's direction, stared into the smoky glare. "Oh, I see we have a representative from Webster's here tonight! Well, good luck with your diploma, sir, but I did mean DONATING." She winked and crossed to center stage. "You . . ." She pointed to the audience. "Are going to buy me." Cheers and hoots spread through the crowd. "What you get is a date with me . . ." She pulled a voucher from her pocket. "A romantic dinner . . ."

Julie leaned forward and smiled. "At the Seven Seas."

"At the Seven Seas . . ." Sheila slid her thumbs beneath the lapel of her crimson jacket. "Followed by some hot dancing at Celebrities, and maybe a bit more . . ." Squeals of delight circulated the room. "Women only, please." She chuckled. "So, what's the first bid?"

"Twenty-five dollars," called a professional-looking woman sitting next to the stage.

"I don't think so!" Sheila feigned insult. "I know some of you have had me for less, but I'm getting my own TV show now, so my price has gone up. Besides . . ." She smiled mischievously. "If you don't come up with more money, I'm gonna 'out' the whole

lot of you on national TV! Prime time!" She turned
to the attractive transgressor and grinned. "That's
when Ma and Pa watch . . ."

The woman was charmed. "One hundred dollars."

"You can do better than that," Sheila challenged
the crowd.

Bids started being called from around the crowded
room. "One-twenty-five. One-fifty. One-seventy-five.
Two hundred . . ."

The last voice was Julie's. Sheila turned in her
direction. "Oh . . . my girlfriend wants a date with
me." She looked out at the audience and smiled.

"Bid it up! Make her pay!"

More calls came from the smoky depths of the
club. "Three hundred. Three-fifty. Four hundred."

"Five hundred." Julie beamed. Katie looked at
her, astonished.

"Seven-fifty."

All heads turned, seeking the source of the
generous bid. Katie and Julie craned around and
spotted Lynn, sitting with Bill in the back of the
room. Lynn looked at Julie and smiled.

Julie felt suddenly uneasy, but also amused at the
prospect of using Lynn's own money to outbid her.
"One thousand."

Lynn casually sipped her wine. "Eleven hundred."

"Twelve hundred," Julie countered.

Lynn didn't miss a beat. "Twenty-five hundred."

Bill stared at Lynn, shocked. Julie leaned back in
her chair, nonplussed. The crowd buzzed with
excitement.

Sheila squinted. "Well, I can't see you . . ." She
tried to block the spotlight with her hand. "But you
sound like a woman with good taste, lots of money,

and no one to spend it on ... Just my type!" She chuckled along with the audience.

Katie glanced at Julie, who looked very uneasy.

"Going once ..." Sheila paced the stage. "Going twice ..."

Julie watched Lynn check her makeup in her compact mirror.

"Sold!" Sheila extended her hands dramatically, playfully preparing to be swept off her feet. "I'm all yours!"

An apprehensive silence filled the room, then erupted into applause as Lynn emerged from the shadows and approached the stage. Sheila turned to Julie, stunned. Things seemed to be happening in slow motion. Julie lit a cigarette ... Lynn reached for the voucher ... The crowd cheered obliviously ...

♥ ♥ ♥

As Julie and Katie approached the dressing room, Sheila bolted into the hall.

"I think somebody likes you ..." Katie jingled.

Sheila brushed past them. "She can't do this to me."

Julie looked to Katie, who only shrugged and began to worry silently.

By the time Julie pushed through the club doors, Sheila was halfway down the block. She considered taking off after her, but the very thought of putting herself in that position made her recoil. She waited for Katie and stared down the street.

The city seemed languid and unrighteous on the damp, moonless night. Its after-midnight citizens wandered, weary, wasted, seemingly blind to each other's dramas. As Katie came through the door, Julie turned to her and spoke in a whisper. "Do you think she does?"

Katie looked perplexed. "Does what?"

"Like her." Julie leaned back against the wall. "You know..."

Katie moved directly in front of her. "Lynn?"

"Stupid idea, right?" Julie pulled a Marlboro from its pack with her lips.

Katie stepped back. "Are you serious?"

"Well..." Julie flipped open her lighter. "She was in the gallery this morning and she bought that sculpture I did of Sheila. Twelve hundred bucks, just like it was nothing."

"Damn."

Julie's flint was dead. "Damn is right. And now, twenty-five hundred bucks for a date with her... What do you think?"

Katie chuckled. "I think she's got a lot of money."

"And apparently she wants to spend it all on Sheila." Julie flicked the lighter with growing futility.

"Sheila does have her charm..."

"How reassuring." She gave up, tucking the lighter and cigarette inside her beat-up Harley Davidson jacket. She snapped the pocket shut, inhaled the scent of the leather, listened for its slight crackle when she moved. She remembered going into the Marnier Pawn Shop to look for a reel-to-reel tape deck and coming out with the jacket instead. The shop's manager, who called herself Regina Gran Marnier, had given Julie an irresistible deal. Julie had known her since junior high, when she was simply Reggie Eldridge, and they'd sort of fooled around one night after dropping off their dates. They'd driven to the beach to watch the sun come up, and ended up drinking a bottle of Mad Dog in the lifeguard stand . . . and somehow kissing. They talked about it several days later, and decided it was an expression of friendship that didn't need to be *analyzed*. After that, they'd drifted apart. Her first kiss . . . She hadn't thought about that in a long time.

"Look . . ." Katie took Julie by the arm. "It doesn't make sense. Sheila's not one to be bothered by someone liking her."

"Yeah." Julie stared down at the wet cobblestones. "That's my job."

"Come on." Katie tugged at her sleeve. "Let's go talk to her."

"Forget it." Julie backed away. "I don't want her raining on my parade all night. I'm going to the club." She wished her lighter was working. "And you?"

"No . . ." Katie checked her watch. "I think I'll go tend to Sheila."

Julie turned and disappeared down the sidewalk. Katie thought she heard her say "Good luck."

Stella's ears perked up as the front door clicked open and closed, but she remained silently roosted in Sheila's lap as Katie passed through the foyer, down the hall, and into the darkened living room. Sheila sat cross-legged on the carpet, leaning back against the sofa. She did not look up.

90

Katie finally broke the silence. "I knew you'd be in the mood to talk, so I thought I'd stop by."

"Where's Julie?" Sheila asked in a whisper.

"She . . . made some comment about the weather and went off to the club." Katie crossed the room toward Sheila. "So, what's going on?"

"Nothing's going on." Sheila scratched Stella's back.

"Let's recap, shall we?" Katie squatted down beside her. "You get the biggest break of your career, and you run out of a business meeting and puke."

"You shouldn't sit like that in your condition."

Katie persisted. "The producers come to your house, and you do your hostess from hell routine."

"What, you were eavesdropping?"

"And now, Lynn Matthews, of all people, donates a shitload of money to *your* favorite cause, and you act like a maniac." She leaned in front of Sheila. "Yes, it's clear to me that nothing's going on."

Sheila shook Stella off of her lap, maneuvered around Katie, and left the room. After several moments, Katie followed. As she approached the stairwell, she heard Sheila shuffling around upstairs in the bedroom. She waited.

Sheila came halfway down the steps and stopped short on the landing. Katie eyed the small, plastic object Sheila was fidgeting with, and almost didn't catch it when Sheila tossed it down to her. It was a single-frame viewfinder, with an amusement park logo etched into the side. "Is this a joke?"

"Look at it," Sheila implored. "Please . . ."

Katie held the tiny lens against her eye and pointed it toward the light. It was a picture of Sheila. She looked about seventeen. She had her arm around a pretty blonde girl, who looked just slightly older. At first, Katie couldn't place the face. Then, she turned to Sheila, shocked. "Lynn?"

Sheila nodded slightly.

"Lynn, as in 'first love Lynn?' "

Sheila stared into space.

"What is going on?"

Sheila came down several steps, then pulled an envelope from the back pocket of her Levi's. She traded it for the viewfinder, and sat down on the stairs.

Katie motioned for Sheila to move over, and sat beside her. She slid the letter from its envelope, unfolded and read it. "You met with her?"

Sheila stared down at the black and white tiles. "I didn't get a chance to."

Katie refolded the note, leaned back against the wall. "Well, it looks like you're getting a second chance."

Sheila twisted the viewfinder chain around her ring finger until it cut off her circulation, then snapped.

Spinning lights and writhing bodies reflected down the length of the mirrored column. Music pounded. Sirens blared. Perched on a stool at the base of the pillar, Julie sat alone. Shot glasses rimmed the perimeter of the small, marble tabletop against which she leaned.

She knocked back a Cuervo and wiped her mouth with her leather sleeve. She didn't even really like tequila. And she hadn't been drunk since college. Not just drunk . . . shitfaced. She was certifiably shitfaced, but why? She'd pondered that all night. Clearly something having to do with Lynn. But what? She didn't really believe Sheila was interested in Lynn, and Lynn being interested in Sheila was unimaginable. So was she just being insecure? Uncharacteristic as that was, it seemed the only acceptable conclusion.

Julie wasn't sure if she was awake or dreaming. It seemed like morning. The sun was pouring in through the glass doors. The seagulls were calling. And, across the room, Stella was hovering in mid-air.

"One of these things is not like the others . . ." She hummed the Sesame Street tune. Her head was pounding. She propped herself up on one elbow, rubbed the slits that were her eyes, looked again. No Stella. She sat up and realized she still had on her boots. She squeezed her forehead, ran a hand through her matted curls. 'Midnight Hairstylist' had outdone herself . . .

From the corner of her eye, she detected Stella gradually levitating above the couch. She twisted out of bed, onto her feet. The room spun clockwise, just a little. She was almost sure she could make it to the couch, but hugging the wall wouldn't be a bad idea.

As she came around the side of the couch, she discovered Sheila lying on the floor. She was on her back, with her legs extended into the air. Atop her feet, a precariously balanced Stella proved her loyalty.

"New Jane Fonda video?" Julie smirked.

"No, my own." Sheila bent her knees. "I call it 'Exercising with Your Children.' " Stella leapt to the floor and ran off.

Julie headed down the hall.

"You got in late last night," Sheila called after her.

"You were awake?"

"You were drunk?"

Julie returned from the bathroom carrying four aspirin and a cup of water. "I'm still drunk . . ." She popped the aspirin into her mouth and washed them down. "And I'm going back to bed."

Sheila heard the thud of Julie dropping onto the mattress and the bang of her boots being kicked to the floor. She wanted to talk to her — needed to. But what would she say? She stared up at the ceiling and prepared her explanation.

A lone ferry glided silently through the inlet. A slight drizzle tapped against the beach house. The wind chimes swayed melodically in the evening breeze.

Sheila wedged her hand down the leg of her

jeans, trying to tuck in the long, white shirt — last summer's line from The Gap men's department. She checked herself in the mirror. Unremarkable, the look she wanted.

She zipped up her pants and slid a thin, black belt through the loops. "If you think you can just waltz in here after a decade . . . a decade and a half really . . . husband in tow, no less . . . you're wrong!"

Stella looked over from the foot of the bed. She knew Sheila must be talking to her, since they were alone in the room, but she didn't recognize any of the words. They weren't the ones for going outside or getting food. She listened more closely as the tirade continued.

"Three weeks ago, *maybe* . . ." Sheila pulled open the armoire and shuffled through her jackets. "But not now. No fucking way." She turned toward Stella. "Isn't that right, Stella?"

Stella wagged her tail half-heartedly. She recognized her name, but the tone sounded alarmingly similar to when she'd last chewed up the couch. Earlier today she'd made off with one of Julie's paintbrushes, but she didn't think anyone had noticed yet. She rolled onto her back and played innocent.

"Sweet girl." Sheila reached for the Gortex windbreaker, then noticed her black suit hanging beside it. Wrapped in plastic, fresh from the dry cleaners. She slid the jacket off its hanger, and held it up against herself in the mirror.

Julie was in a funk. She'd been holed up in her

studio since she'd climbed out of bed — had gone through seven C.D.'s, four espressos, and had little to show for it. She liked the two faces in profile, her hands holding Sheila's face. But that design had been accomplished days ago. Today she'd simply done battle with ornery tinctures that seemed unwilling to bend to her creative impulse, determined to evade her imagination.

She paced the room, staring willfully at the canvas. Something was missing. A vibrance in the touch of the hands to the cheeks. A passion in the lock of the eyes. A purity of moment ... like the photo she kept on the nightstand ...

As she came around the corner into the bedroom, she discovered Sheila struggling to apply mascara in front of the upright mirror. She leaned against the doorframe with one arm and glared at her. "Makeup?"

Sheila glanced sideways at Julie's reflection, but did not turn around.

"Well ..." Julie couldn't help recognizing the elegant black suit, silk shirt, Italian loafers. Sheila had bought the outfit in Key West last October, for their anniversary dinner. "Introducing bachelorette number one." She gestured broadly toward Sheila. "Bachelorette, please tell us bit about yourself, your plans for the future ..."

"Do you mind?" Sheila slowly screwed the top on the mascara.

"I mind a helluva lot."

"Look ..." She turned to face Julie. "You can have a date with me anytime."

"This isn't about the date."

Sheila loosed a charming grin. "The makeup?" She twirled the mascara tube like a tiny baton.

Julie stared, unamused.

"You know . . ." Sheila glanced perfunctorily at her watch. "I'm on my way out."

Julie pushed off from the doorframe and crossed toward Sheila. "I'm acutely aware of that."

"Please . . ." Sheila reached and put her hands on Julie's shoulders. "We'll talk later, okay?"

They hadn't talked all day, but Julie knew she was equally responsible for that. She took a step backward. "I'll wait up." She turned and headed down the stairs at a rapid clip.

Sheila watched Julie's silhouette recede against the colorful patchwork of stained-glass that spanned the stairwell. For a moment, she felt relieved. Then, slowly, it began to hit her. The day had seemed to drag on forever, but now there was nothing left standing between her and this dinner, between her and Lynn . . .

She broke into a sudden sweat and her head began to pound. She steadied herself against the armoire and rubbed her eyes, desperate to halt the rush of images washing over her. Not again, she thought, not now. But it was too late. The room blurred and metamorphosed, and she slipped helplessly into the past . . .

Green and yellow balloons hung clustered along shiny streams of ribbon. A macramé sleeve scraped through pink-icing rosebuds. A flame dipped to ignite twenty thin wicks. A plateful of Angelfood was passed toward her. She could hear Lynn's voice singing softly, "Happy birthday to you, happy birthday to you . . ."

She basked in Lynn's attention. They were living a defining moment, and she knew she'd always remember it. She closed her eyes, made a wish, blew breath against fire. Crystal goblets clinked in praise of friendship. Ripple poured freely from a gallon jug . . . warmed their bellies . . . pulsed through them.

Leaning side by side against the sink, they scraped cold lasagna off their plates and struggled playfully for control of the spray nozzle. It whipped about wildly and quickly drenched them both. Lynn backed Sheila against the counter and held her there. The nozzle dropped. The laughing stopped.

"Happy birthday," Sheila sang in a whisper, "to me . . ." She leaned forward and kissed Lynn. Quick and casual.

They exchanged half smiles. Rain washed down the windows.

"Happy . . . birth . . ." Lynn faltered under Sheila's stare. Their movement toward each other was tentative, painstaking. Their lips drew together, opened, tasted. Their bodies locked and rocked rhythmically.

Lightning flashed and thunder crashed.

"No!" Lynn shook free and frantically wiped her lips, desperate to cleanse their transgression.

Sheila stood frozen against the counter. "Lynn . . ."

"Get out . . ." Lynn backed into the hallway and pointed a trembling finger toward the door.

"Lynn, please . . ." Sheila matched Lynn's steps, reaching out for her. "Please . . ."

"Get out . . ." Lynn flung the door open. The wind gusts muffled her cries and lashed blonde hair across her anguished face.

Sheila felt the stinging pelt of rain as she backed into the downpour. "But I love you . . ." She threw herself against the slamming door. Her body throbbed and burned as she collapsed to the ground. Sobbing and choking on mucus, she screamed into the darkness, "I thought you loved me . . ."

♥ ♥ ♥

A distant siren echoed across the water as Sheila crossed through the gazebo toward the floating restaurant. She descended a ramp and entered the bar area. Neon-lit tanks of tropical fish lined the planked walls. The maitre 'd nodded his usual hello and pointed her toward the upper deck.

She spiraled up a Plexiglas stairway, through lush, imported foliage. She spotted Lynn at a table by the window, and paused behind a palm. Lynn looked almost surreal, her ivory skin set against the dark sky, the city lights cresting behind her . . .

Sheila straightened her jacket and ran a hand through her hair, which was stiff with gel. She mustered a confident stride and approached the table, tracked by Lynn's cerulean eyes.

"Can I get you ladies something to drink?" No sooner had Sheila sat down than Keith stood above her. He'd worked at the restaurant for years, and served her regularly.

"Two glasses of Pouilly-Fuisse," Lynn answered authoritatively, before Sheila got a chance.

Keith waited for Sheila's nod, then disappeared.

Sheila leaned back in her chair. "What . . . no more Ripple?"

Lynn sipped her water. "You know . . . some of the

most charming things come out of your mouth, Sheila." She dabbed her lips with a napkin. "They'll play well in the show."

Sheila stared, dumbfounded and stung by Lynn's patronizing tone.

"So, how do you find the terms of the contract?" Sheila leaned forward. "I find them outrageous."

"What can I bring you ladies for dinner?" Keith set two glasses of wine on the table.

They glanced down at their unopened menus. "I'll just have the usual." Sheila forced a smile.

"Yes, the usual sounds good." Lynn handed both menus to Keith. "I'll have that too." She waited till he was out of earshot, then leaned very deliberately toward Sheila. "So . . . what are we having?"

Lynn's smile undid Sheila in an instant. The look in her eyes was so familiar, it was as if no time had passed. Sheila knew she could crack a joke and make everything be okay. They could reminisce, share stories. She'd always wanted to show Lynn Santorini . . .

Feeling suddenly nauseous, she averted her eyes and sat back in her chair.

"So . . ." Lynn hadn't counted on Sheila resisting her smile. She resumed a business-like demeanor. "You were saying there was a problem with the terms?"

Sheila picked up her salad fork and began tapping it against the table.

"You couldn't have failed to notice how favorable they are . . ."

A moment ago, Sheila was ready to whisk this woman off to the Mediterranean. Now she just wanted to fling a fork at her. "This was a mistake."

She tossed the fork down on the table. "I'll get you your twenty-five hundred dollars back and you can talk to me at the next business meeting. No charge."

"I'm not here to talk about business." Lynn lowered her voice. "I'm here to talk about you and me."

Sheila was outraged. "There is no you and me! Remember? Never was!"

Lynn glanced around nervously. "Look . . ." She folded her hands on the table. "I've been thinking about this for a long time, and I'm prepared to acknowledge that I didn't handle our . . . situation . . . in an appropriate manner. I just didn't know how to deal with your attraction to me."

"*My* attraction to *you*?"

"Yes." Lynn's tone was matter-of-fact. "I knew that it existed, and I could handle it to a certain point. But I couldn't deal with you starting to act like you were . . ."

"Your boyfriend?"

Lynn glared at Sheila. "You WEREN'T my boyfriend."

"That's right. I was your GIRLFRIEND!"

"You shouldn't have kissed me . . ." Lynn's voice was shaky. "Everything would have been all right if you just hadn't kissed me."

Sheila leaned forward on one elbow and pointed a finger at Lynn. "You kissed me back."

Lynn looked away, unable to face Sheila's accusing stare.

Sheila leaned closer. "Tell me you kissed me back, Lynn."

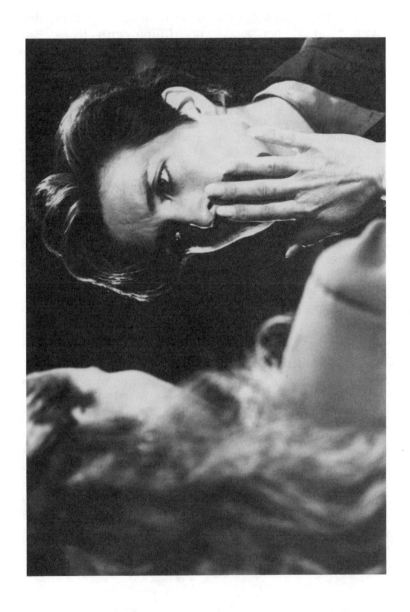

The city lights appeared to blur and splinter, and Lynn realized her eyes were filling with tears. She glanced at Sheila, then grabbed her purse and fled down the steps.

She traveled at a fast clip — past the trellised gazebo, through the shipyard, into the maze of docks. Tugboats rocked and creaked in their slips, like burly watchmen. The night seemed alive. She paused to catch her breath.

"TELL ME!" Sheila's voice came suddenly from behind her, and she felt herself being spun around by the arm. "Tell me, Lynn."

Before realizing what she was doing, Lynn reached and pressed her fingers against Sheila's lips to silence her. The intimacy of the action jolted them both. Their eyes locked. For a moment, neither of them moved.

Sheila slowly reached up and clutched Lynn's fingers. Her skin felt soft. Smelled faintly like rose. "Instinct."

Lynn looked at her own hand wrapped in Sheila's, and images rolled unbidden through her mind. Eighth grade. School trip. Back of the bus. Nighttime. The motor hummed and rocked them gently. They'd held hands, fallen asleep holding each other. The first of many times they would. So innocent they never talked about it. And so guilty, Lynn hadn't once mentioned it to Dr. VanDerhoff in three years of Tuesday sessions.

"I have to go." She pulled away, unable to hold herself together a moment longer. She could feel Sheila's eyes on her back as she fled, and she slipped out of sight behind the dockmaster's office. The

Nutcracker Suite drifted unseasonably from an open window, and she tried to lose herself in its melody, but could not slow the race of her heart.

♥ ♥ ♥

"You're in early." Bill muted the Movie of the Week and looked over from the bed. Lynn shut the door behind her, took off her jacket and hung it in the closet. Something was wrong. She wasn't biting. "So . . ." He tried again. "Did you get your money's worth?" She glared at him, eyes like ice and fire at the same time. He unwedged a cigarette pack from his shirt pocket. "Hey, I was just joking . . ."

Lynn slipped into the bathroom without a word. He jumped up and got there just in time to hear the lock click shut. "You know, every time you see Sheila, you end up in a shitty mood!" His words were drowned out by the sound of running bath water.

He grabbed his lighter off the beveled glass ledge. No fluid. He tossed it down and tucked the cigarette back in his pocket. He glanced at the sculpture of the woman, prominently displayed on the ledge. It had an odd sense of presence — substance and texture. An unconventional choice for Lynn, given her leanings toward the two-dimensional. He felt a sense of unease, but refused to name it.

♥ ♥ ♥

"So, did you earn your twenty-five hundred bucks?" Julie sat on the steps, legs pulled up and hugged in her arms.

Sheila found herself standing in the foyer, not sure what time it was or how she'd gotten home. She kicked the door shut. "I could think of better ways to spend an evening." The best defense was a good offense. She took off toward the kitchen.

Julie found Sheila staring blankly into the refrigerator. She stood in the doorway, arms folded. "Do we need to have a talk about Lynn?"

"There's nothing to talk about."

"I think maybe there is."

Sheila slammed the refrigerator door and brushed past Julie.

Julie heard the glass doors slide open and shut. She tried to calm herself down. Counted to ten. Twenty. Thirty. It wasn't working.

The frigid water stung Julie's legs as she trudged full-speed into the bay. An oar smashed wildly in front of her. She grabbed hold of it, yanked it against her body, held it still. "What's happening to us?"

Sheila stared at the mountain, silent. Water lapped against the boat.

"You know, I'm used to this little boat thing of yours . . . but I never expected this." Julie shoved the oar away from her. "Not from you." She turned and made her way back to shore, accompanied by the smack of wood against water.

Several dogs yelped in protection of their property as Sheila cut across two yards and wound toward the wood garage. Her yellow raincoat sliced the misty gray of the morning. Her boots collected shiny shreds of wet grass. Hot coffee splashed onto her hands from two Brew-Ha-Ha cups.

The 1960 Mercedes sat elevated on cement blocks. Welding sparks sprayed from beneath the back fender, where a pair of legs extended off the edge of a dolly. Sheila set the cups on the trunk and squatted down. "You know, one of these days you're gonna blow this thing up." The masked welder turned Sheila's way. "At least you'll go out with a bang!" She grabbed the coffees and stepped back as the dolly slid out from under the car.

Katie lifted her face-plate and pointed the torch toward the cups. "Need a warm-up?" She chuckled.

Sheila pulled down her rain hood and grinned. "Your decaf, madam."

"Jesus Sheila . . ." Katie reached for the cup. "You look like shit."

"Thanks for noticing."

Katie sipped her coffee. "Sleep on the couch?"

Sheila grimaced.

"So, how'd it go?"

Sheila turned and ambled over to the workbench. *"I'm prepared to acknowledge that I didn't handle our . . . situation . . . in an appropriate manner."* She fumbled through a toolbox and pulled out an ice pick. "And, I put MASCARA on for this woman!" She drove the pick into the bench.

"Put that down. It's not a toy." Katie sipped her coffee, eyed Sheila suspiciously. "Did you wear your black suit?"

Sheila shifted uncomfortably. "Yeah . . . so?"

"Temptation . . ."

"Ends in 'shun' . . ."

"Class dismissed." Katie pulled her face-plate down and reached for the torch.

"She's fucking with my head . . ."

Katie lifted the mask. "I think you're doing some of that yourself."

"Oh yeah?" Sheila approached her, poised for battle. "What else do you think?"

"Oh, you wanna know what I think?"

114

"Yeah." What she really wanted was for Katie to validate the notion of Lynn's culpability, but she knew that wasn't how Katie worked. She pulled over a step ladder and sat down.

"Very well, then. My assessment is that you've been having a long-term relationship with a photograph." Katie feigned contemplation. "Successful, but somehow . . . warped." Her flippant tone became more serious. "The absent one can do no wrong. It requires nothing of you. No problems, no negotiating. Nice and safe. The perfect relationship!"

Sheila stared down at the cup she was tearing to pieces.

"And Sheila, at the rate you're going, you'll soon be having that same 'perfect' relationship with a photograph of Julie."

Sheila looked up. "Touché . . ."

"Do you know what your problem is?" Katie wasn't finished.

Take a number, Sheila thought.

"You have a Snow White complex."

Sheila stood up. "You sound like a fortune cookie." She paced and fought the urge to put her hands over her ears and hum loudly.

"There you've been . . . secretly waiting all this time for Lynn to ride up on some big, white horse, and whisk you away to happily-ever-after-land."

"I have not!" Sheila looked over at Katie. "I wanted to be the one riding the white horse . . ." She gripped imaginary reins and trotted in place with a silly grin.

Don Quixote miscast as Prince Charming, Katie

thought. "You're so pathetic." She slid her mask down and picked up the torch.

"That's no news flash." Sheila stared out at the rain.

Katie flipped up the face plate and stared intently at Sheila. "Go home." She laid back on the dolly and slid under the car.

Sheila lifted her hood and ventured out into the storm. She would take the beach route home.

What came to mind was the fullness of Julie's laugh. Her reverent spirit. Her open heart. The strength and tenderness of her touch. The delicious curve of her collar bone.

Sheila trudged through the rain-pocked sand. She picked up a starfish and ran her fingers across its knobby shell. Her Dad had told her that a starfish can detach any leg and form a second starfish. She still wasn't sure if it was true, but she felt a new appreciation for the concept.

She tossed the starfish into the water. Katie was right, of course. Sheila wanted to spend the rest of her life with Julie. She would do nothing to jeopardize that. She felt an odd sense of relief, as if she'd made a decision.

A mesmerizing rain tapped at the windows, casting shifting patterns of light and shadow across the studio walls, along the contours of Julie's skin. She sat on the edge of her drafting table, legs dangling. She listened to the rain's hum, tired of all her tapes and CD's. She shook tiny paint chips off her woolen socks, and watched them float to the floor like confetti. She was out of cigarettes.

"Julie . . ." Sheila's voice came with a tentative knock.

"I'm working." She stared at the door, half-hoping to fail in her rebuff. But it did not open.

She hopped down from the table, grabbed her palette and brush. Rain-shadows slid like dark tears down the canvas. She had captured the look, the engagement of eyes. But the image haunted rather than pleased her, begging twistedly for transformation . . .

She put brush to palette, mixing a smooth golden swirl, and returned to work with new resolve.

Sheila rowed furiously, a solitary yellow dot wrapped in a blanket of gray fog. She imagined tracking Lynn down and confronting her. All the things she'd never gotten to say pulsed through her mind like a migraine, and she fantasized their outpouring on a defenseless Lynn . . . But part of her was afraid she'd never see Lynn again. And the other part was afraid they were one conversation away from making love.

♥ ♥ ♥

Katie and Julie arrived late and lost their usual table. They were escorted to a small booth against the wall, stage left. Katie indulged in a Virgin Mary, double celery. Julie abstained.

Sheila was mid-act. "I feel the need to chip away

at a little lesbian folklore here. Partly, perhaps, because I just can't live up to the standard it suggests. It goes something like this..." Her voice took on a mimicking tone. "When I was first with a woman, I knew *instinctively* what to do..."

Lynn watched Sheila from the back of the room. She ran her finger along the edge of her wine glass, and pretended not to notice Bill looking at her from the corner of his eye.

"These days it's gotten so complicated." Sheila pulled the microphone from its stand and launched into an argument with herself. "You be on top... No, I was on top last time, remember, before we bought the house... Well, okay, but I love it with candles... Yeah, well flickering candles give me seizures... Then at least we have to use latex... Geez, am I dating the daughter of the Man From Glad?" Sheila swung her arms into the air. "Take me to the convent!" She paused, smiled dreamily. "And who knows... maybe Julie Andrews will be there..."

She paced the stage, waiting for the laughter to die down. She spotted Julie and sauntered toward her. "You know, up until nineteen-seventy-three, homosexuality was a diagnosable illness..." Julie sat back and crossed her arms. Sheila grinned her most dapper grin. "You could wake up Monday morning, gaze lovingly at that sexy woman lying beside you, pick up the phone, and call in 'gay' for work!" The crowd roared, but Julie sat stiff, unresponsive. Katie noticed the exchange. Sheila crossed back to center stage. "Ah, the good old days." She clipped the microphone back into its stand. "Thanks. You've been a great audience."

As the crowd began to file out of the club, Sheila crossed toward Julie and Katie's table. Abruptly, a hand grabbed her shoulder from behind.

"I'd like to speak with you." Lynn's tone was urgent.

Sheila nervously glanced in Julie's direction.

Julie watched Lynn pull Sheila into a huddle against the wall. "Am I crazy or is something going on between them?"

Katie chomped nervously on her celery stick. "What kind of something?"

"I think Lynn wants to sow her oats a little, and I think she wants to use Sheila to do it."

"Well . . ." Katie stalled. "What has Sheila said?"

"She won't talk to me."

Katie fished an ice cube from her glass and cracked it between her teeth. "Yeah, she can be pretty uncommunicative at times."

Julie shifted to get a better view.

"I can't talk to you anymore." Sheila backed away from Lynn, under the weight of Julie's stare.

As Lynn reached for her, Bill suddenly planted himself between them. "Are you ready to go?"

"Uh, no . . ." Lynn glanced at Sheila. "I think I'll just stay here for a while."

Bill looked around the club. "There's nothing else going on here."

"Well, I feel like staying anyway." Lynn glared at him.

"I think it's time to leave." He took her by the arm. "Goodnight, Sheila." Lynn glanced briefly at Sheila, then yanked her arm free and headed for the door. Bill followed quickly behind her.

As the house lights came up, Sheila caught sight of Katie and Julie exiting into the night. She sank into a booth and watched the club spit its last few patrons onto the street. Busboys began scooping glasses and ashtrays into plastic bins. A vacuum cleaner came on in the back of the room.

"I think you're just wonderful!" the lighting technician called down from the rafters.

Sheila looked up and mustered a weak smile. "Manna from heaven."

♥ ♥ ♥

Lynn remained tight-lipped all the way home, replaying the scene in her mind and wishing she'd handled it differently. She jumped out of the car as soon as it pulled up in front of the hotel. Bill chased her across the lobby and made it into the elevator just as the doors slid closed.

By the time they reached the penthouse, Lynn thought she'd explode. She shot into the suite like a bullet. "I'd appreciate it if you would not embarrass me like that in the future!"

Bill pushed through the door behind her. "Are you suggesting that it's a crime for me to ask you to accompany me home? After all, you ARE my wife!"

Lynn kept moving, did not respond.

"Case in point! You see Sheila, you act like a bitch."

"You don't understand . . ." She circled to the far side of the table.

"You're right, and I'd appreciate an explanation."

She snapped open her briefcase and shuffled randomly through some papers. "Not now."

Bill reached across the table. "NOW!" He slammed the case shut. "What is going on with you two?"

"I don't know."

"I think you do."

"I don't want to talk about it." Not yet, not with you.

Bill walked over to the balcony and stared out into the night. "Well then, I'll do the talking." He realized he wasn't sure what he wanted to say. How much to say. He watched the headlights streaking endlessly across the Lion's Bay Bridge, and remembered crossing it himself on the way in from the airport. How differently things were evolving than what he'd anticipated. "This whole situation is making me very uncomfortable," he began slowly, "and I'm having second thoughts about moving forward with the show."

"Oh, really?" Lynn turned and glared at him. "Well, as I recall, this business belongs to both of us. And if you back out of this project . . . I'll just do it without you."

"And what about our marriage?" He stalked toward her, enraged. "Will you do THAT without me too?" He didn't expect an answer. Didn't even want one. They'd been through variations of this conversation before, always colluding somehow to circumvent its inevitable conclusion. Lynn complied, as always, layering stone-faced silence over her anguish. Bill exited on cue, slamming the door behind him.

"Trouble in paradise . . ." Eliza mixed a distracted martini, her hazel eyes tracking Sheila, who slinked solo through the sweaty, wound-up, Friday night mob. From her post at the bar, Eliza bore vigilant witness to the club's ceaseless drama — a mixed spectacle of passion's headlong rush from kindling to burnout. She'd long ago concluded that it smacked of soap opera at worst, real opera at best. And the fat lady was singing for Sheila now. Eliza was sure. She saw all the signs. She'd also driven Julie home the other night, after finding her out back by the dumpster, crying.

Sheila felt the floor pounding beneath her feet as she rounded the balcony and spotted Julie and Katie in their usual corner. She paused in the shadows, undetected, and stared down at the shape-shifting mass below. Lynn danced among the crowd. No . . . that wasn't Lynn. The woman sitting by the column was. Maybe. No, not her either. The more Sheila looked, the more candidates she found, and her guts twisted at the sudden recollection of years spent mistaking women everywhere for Lynn. It was a cycle of surprise, disappointment, relief, and devastation. A slow, steady drip of brutality.

She released her white-knuckled grip on the rail, stepped back and ran a damp hand through her hair. She felt an intense, almost desperate desire to lure Julie home and make love to her. To anchor herself in the rhythm of Julie's breath, collapse into her gaze, and forever renounce this curriculum of ruin. But tempered by guilt, she approached Julie sheepishly and slipped a nonchalant arm around her. "Wanna dance?"

Julie stiffened and looked away. Silence briskly carved a prison and bound them in its corrosive grip. Katie vacuumed up the last of her Perrier through a tiny straw. "Well, I'm going to take myself home now, ladies. Goodnight." She didn't wait for a response.

Sheila leaned against the railing and locked her eyes on the grid of spinning lights. "Look, there's something I have to talk to you about."

"Lynn . . ."

"No. Well . . . yeah."

Julie twisted her cufflink. "I already know."

"What?" Sheila turned to her. "Katie told you?"

"Oh my God . . . I knew it!" Julie pressed both hands against her temples. "I fucking knew it . . ."

"I don't understand . . ."

Sheila seemed sincere, and Julie wondered for a moment if she was losing her mind. Had she built an entire scenario with materials of her own making? The misconstruction of nuance and innuendo? The fabrication of reality? Could such a tentative structure withstand the huff-and-puff of imminent invalidation? And why resist invalidation, when what she most wanted was for Sheila to prove her wrong, bring a different truth to light.

Julie forced her eyes to meet Sheila's, then abruptly zeroed in on a target behind her. A tremor of anger shook through her. "That's it! I'm outta here!" She pivoted, knocking two women against the wall in her bolt for the stairs.

Sheila spun to look behind her. "Shit . . ."

"Bad timing?" Lynn read panic in Sheila's eyes and immediately regretted her acerbic tone.

"Unbelievable . . ." Sheila stepped back as Lynn

moved forward. "Look, I can't talk to you right now. I gotta go." She dodged into the crowd.

Lynn took off after Sheila, who rushed down the dim stairwell jumping three steps at a time. Lynn lunged and grabbed her sleeve from behind. "Sheila, please . . ."

Sheila shook her arm free. Not turning around, but not leaving either.

Lynn's palms felt moist as she rubbed them together and tried to compose herself. *What am I doing?* She descended several steps. Her chest pulsed hypnotically, resonating with the steady dance beat. Her heart seemed to pound inside her ears and echo through her body. *What am I doing?* Her words were quickly conceived and delivered. "I kissed you back."

The relief was immediate . . . physical. Complete like orgasm. "That's what I came here to say . . . and now that I've said it, I can leave." She brushed past Sheila and merged into the lobby crowd.

Sheila spotted Lynn halfway down the side alley. A peculiar image — larger-than-life Lynn dwarfed by garbage dumpsters. For a moment, Sheila felt a familiar sense of protectiveness toward her — a terrifying impulse, which she quickly transformed into rage. "Still running?"

The question smacked of challenge. Lynn stopped, pressed her manicured hands against the cool brick of the club's exterior. "What more do you want from me?"

Sheila strode resolutely toward her. "Apologize! Grovel! Suffer like I did!"

"I have." Lynn felt oddly relieved by Sheila's sarcasm. It was a comfortable ring to spar in. And Dr. VanDerhoff had explained to her that sarcasm was merely a form of "artful uproar" — a diversionary tactic used to deflect attention from feelings of vulnerability. She studied Sheila and watched for uproar.

Sheila squirmed under Lynn's gaze. "Is that all you have to say?"

Not exactly artful . . .

"Do you know how many letters I wrote you?"

Rhetorical, but Lynn had the answer. "Eleven. Not including the ones you never sent."

Momentarily disarmed, Sheila leaned back against the wall. Lynn was right. Eleven letters. One per week, the maximum allowed by her treatment plan, sent faithfully each Thursday from the Bainbridge Hospital psych unit. She'd agreed to stop all attempts to contact Lynn as a condition of her release, professional consensus having ruled it a "serious impediment" to her recovery. The truth was, Lynn had not responded to a single letter. After the first month or so, Sheila had been writing solely to quell her own demons.

But she kept writing, sometimes several letters a day, for almost two years after that — tucking the letters away in secret shame, maintaining a warped connection to Lynn in the only way she could fathom. Until the eve of her twenty-second birthday, when she resolved to move on with her life and conclude the strange season of pain. She collected the letters, which now numbered in the hundreds, piled them neatly outside her apartment building, and set them on fire. She wrote that night in her journal:

"Now all you are is a stain in my parking lot." She never mentioned it to her therapist, who'd already emphasized that fire was not an "appropriate vent for hostility." But this time she hadn't felt hostile. It was an act of resignation which, she would discover in the years to come, fell miserably short of resolution.

Sheila wedged her boot into a crack in the pavement. The night felt cold. She looked at Lynn — the villain, the stranger. "I hate you for what you did to me."

Lynn responded with strategic indignation, directly proportional to her sense of guilt. "You hate me because I didn't understand? You hate me because I wasn't as *evolved* as you? Or perhaps you just hate me because you didn't get what you wanted." She couldn't let Sheila's stunned expression impede her momentum. "You're not the only one who lost something. This happened to me too, you know."

"Yeah? Well, you're the one that *made* it happen!" Sheila's rage boomeranged instantly, squarely cracking her own armor and liberating utter devastation. "Jesus, Lynn . . . you have no idea how much I loved you."

"Yes, I do."

"Did you . . . back then?"

Lynn nodded a painful confession.

Sheila felt infuriated, and vindicated, and relieved. "Why didn't you say anything?"

"I was scared . . ."

"So was I, but *YOU* went running!"

"I didn't know what else to do . . ." It was an admission of failure, after years of mute self-recrimination. And what failure could be worse than lacking the conviction to love? Lynn felt an uncharacteristic spill of tears down her cheeks. She turned her face to the wall. "I'm sorry..." She smacked her hands against the brick. "I'm sorry..."

Sheila felt an immediate collapse of the distance between them. Her body physically ached at the sight and sound of Lynn's grief. Somehow, despite all the brutality, their union had endured, fragile but intact. *This* Lynn, unraveling before her eyes, was friend. Family.

Sheila approached slowly, turned back, approached again. "It's okay..." She touched Lynn's shoulder. Her hair. "Lynn..." She gently urged Lynn's face away from the wall. "It's okay."

In the amber street light, Lynn's eyes looked like slate gray discs. Sheila looked right through them, as she always had. Neither of them would remember who moved toward who, and neither would forget the stunning meeting of their breath, as their lips brushed, then pushed together.

Sheila stepped back, momentarily overwhelmed by a fleeting recognition of the tragedy she was about to invite into her life. But this woman before her held a piece of her heart that starved for life... and in that moment, weakened like Achilles with Lynn at her heel, she could see no further.

Lynn reached for Sheila, her body crushing inhibitions as quickly as her mind issued them. Years of rich fantasy now prompted possibility — agonizing and thrilling in equal measure.

Sheila rolled into Lynn's embrace like a homecoming. She felt the warm press of her weight, the dampness of lingering tears. Lynn's scent familiar, beckoning her to travel back in time. She

ran the tip of her tongue along the soft curve of Lynn's neck, across her jawline . . . intercepting a tear and tracing its salty path upward. She held Lynn's face with both hands. "Is it you . . .?"

Lynn closed her eyes, spoke Sheila's name and surrendered to what felt like destiny. She felt Sheila's thumb gently crossing her mouth, and she parted her lips — just slightly — so her tongue might run across Sheila's skin. The most sensual thing she'd ever done, that tiny act. At last . . . the taste of Sheila.

Their hands traveled to each other's hair and took hold. Their mouths pushed together deeply, feeding on a forgotten passion. Captivating and chaotic. Sublime and surreal.

Sheila's breath caught, frozen in the moment. Sandwiched between Lynn and the wall, she could feel the curve of a pubis seeking refuge in her own, pressing her through the cloth of two pairs of pants. She existed in pure sensation as Lynn's hands slid down her shoulders . . . passed willfully across her breasts. Her collar was being unbuttoned, her shoulders exposed. She felt skin against her chest, then burning breath.

Emboldened by Sheila's soft moans and the intense ache of her own body, Lynn pinned Sheila's wrists against the wall, felt the scrape of cool brick against her knuckles. Her tongue rounded Sheila's nipple, retreating teasingly as it strained for her, its hardness inviting her lips to fasten, to suck. And when they did, locking onto Sheila starved and unrestrained, Lynn dissolved into an unknowing of where she left off and Sheila began. She longed to swallow Sheila whole . . . keep her inside forever . . . capture the shiver that shook them both, as her hands traveled down the firm slope of Sheila's belly, unbuttoned her jeans, found her hot and soaked in the broth of their frantic foreplay.

"What are you doing?" Sheila jolted back abruptly, smacked by another reality. She fumbled to fasten her pants, keeping her eyes fixed on Lynn. "What are you doing . . .?"

"Being who I am . . ." Lynn fell mute, shocked by her own declaration. And staggeringly relieved. Her self-imposed laws of concealment and camouflage had claimed a savage toll over the years, bequeathing only the harsh lesson that silence was an eloquent form of lying. But now she'd been set free. The truth was no longer dark and unrevealed. How could it be, when her fingers were slippery and perfumed with Sheila . . .

"Oh, this is who you are?" Though Sheila had waited years for this naming, she cringed as it occurred in her presence. It felt unexpectedly dangerous. "Does your husband know that?" She hurriedly buttoned her shirt.

"Don't patronize me, Sheila." Lynn was resolute. "We haven't had a marriage for years." This, too, she spoke for the first time — with understanding and without shame.

Sheila paced to discharge the energy pumping through her. "So now you just go around kissing women?"

"No . . ." Lynn grabbed Sheila and held her still. "Just you." Sheila turned away. Lynn moved in front of her, squeezed both her hands. "Just you . . ."

Eager strips of blue, pink, and orange graduated from the darkness and ribboned across the morning sky. The tide pulled itself back from the dock. The herons waded for breakfast. Julie crushed a cigarette onto the patio and wrapped her arms around herself for warmth. Disheveled and exhausted, dressed in last night's clothes, she squeezed herself hard just to feel something. She dug her nails into her palms and resolved to stay sane.

The night had been filled with haunting premonitions. An eruption of images. Irrepressible and unbearable. Plans and decisions had spewed rapidly and in all directions, ultimately negating each other and immobilizing her. She heard the front door open and close. Stella barked, footsteps came down the hall. She could feel Sheila's presence, but did not turn around. "Where the hell have you been?"

Sheila felt a wave of nausea roll through her. She'd counted on Julie being asleep. She needed more time to think, regretted coming home, was afraid she might throw up. "We ... have to talk." She planted herself in the leather armchair.

Julie turned slowly and spoke with menacing restraint. "You're right about that." She stepped into the living room and grabbed her cigarette pack off the table. Empty. She threw it back down. "You were with Lynn, weren't you?"

Sheila was eye level with Julie's waist. She felt like a child preparing for reprimand. "Yes." She tried desperately to conjure self-righteousness, but found only shame, confusion and regret.

Julie pinched a half-smoked cigarette from the pile in the ashtray, lit it, stared at the glowing ash. "Did you sleep with her?" She launched the interrogation in earnest.

Sheila stiffened and tried to compose an articulate, if not acceptable, explanation.

"Answer me, dammit!"

"No ... I didn't sleep with her."

"I don't believe you."

Sheila looked Julie in the eye. "I'm telling you the truth ..."

"The *truth*?" Julie shook her head, disgusted. "I know the truth!" She grabbed a handful of fan mail from the table. "Everyone thinks you're sooo fuuucking wonderful, but I know the truth ..." She rashly flung the letters at Sheila, hitting her in the face. "You're a fucking liar and a coward!"

Sheila jumped from the chair and headed toward the back deck.

Julie spun around, but did not follow. "That boat's not gonna take you anywhere!"

Sheila stepped outside.

"You walk out on this conversation and it'll be the last one we have . . ." Julie couldn't believe what she heard herself saying. Things were escalating so quickly. How had they gotten to this point?

The ultimatum hung in the air, painfully, for what felt like a long time. Sheila knew Julie was telling the truth. It was what she respected most about her. She turned around, slowly, not ready to lose Julie just yet.

Julie's expression was hard. It did not betray her relief. "Ever since you met *Lynn,* you've been acting weird."

Sheila dug her hands into her front pockets. "What did Katie tell you?"

"She didn't tell me anything."

Sheila knew she shouldn't have questioned that. Katie was a friend to both of them. But a part of her wished Katie had spilled everything, spared her the violence of confession. She crossed the room and reached for Julie.

"Don't." Julie flinched. Her jaw trembled.

Sheila withdrew her hand. She knew they were both thinking the same thing. This hand was last laid upon Lynn. The devastation in Julie's eyes was unbearable. Sheila sat on the armchair's edge and stared at the rug. "Look, I didn't just meet Lynn . . ."

Julie mashed her cigarette in the brass ashtray and leaned back onto the couch. The deception went deeper than she'd imagined.

"I know her from a long time ago . . ." Sheila stuttered and searched for words. "She just showed up out of nowhere and caught me completely unprepared."

Julie turned to her. "Unprepared for what?"

"She was my best friend . . ."

"So? Why all the mystery?"

Sheila was at a loss for words. In her entire adult life, she'd only discussed this with Katie, and then not in detail. It had been her private melodrama, that singular circumstance to which she attributed all subsequent failings, and successes. Even her humor drew from taproots grounded deep in this ancient pain. Yet, in retrospect, her epic seemed obscenely ordinary. And wholly uncomplicated. "I was in love . . . and she wasn't."

Although Sheila had never said so directly, Julie had always believed herself to be Sheila's first and only *real* love — a belief Sheila fueled rather than disputed, hoping to rewrite the story of her own heart. But now the ghost had resurrected, manifested, drunk Riesling on their back deck. And Julie had not only unwittingly welcomed the interloper, she'd embraced the insanity of distrusting her own intuition.

Julie's fingers recoiled, scratching along the chintz fabric of the couch. She noticed the green paint stain and remembered the thrill of Sheila's homecoming. She felt as if, since then, she'd been thrust into a life uncharted and not her own. Her fate suddenly rode on a single question. "And now?"

Hoping to buy time, Sheila watched a sea plane travel toward the mountain and pretended to wait for the noise to die down. When it did, silence encroached rapidly, and Sheila knew that if she did not speak soon her muteness would do all the talking. She struggled to dislodge the words from her throat. "I don't know."

Julie spoke in a whisper, almost to herself. "You don't know?"

Sheila could neither watch nor turn away from the pain and rage ravaging her lover's face.

Julie closed her eyes and felt a tear drip onto her hand. "You don't know..." Her voice drifted into resignation. She understood immediately, entirely, the demon she faced. It was love. The kind of love that hibernates in the soul and reigns over all else. Sheila's love for Lynn.

Julie formulated the simple, unaskable question. "What about us...?"

Sheila caught her own reflection in Julie's dark eyes, and like a modern-day Dorian Gray, she watched her image transform into something perverse and detestable. Only a single truth tempered her self-loathing, perhaps even redeemed her. She loved both of them, really loved them, in ways impossible to compare. Choosing between them was as inconceivable as it was inevitable. But for now, there was only one honest answer. "I don't know..."

Julie realized she couldn't fight this fight. It was Sheila's battle, not hers. She rose slowly.

Sheila stared into space and wished she were invisible. She wanted to call out as Julie left the room, but could find no justification for stopping her. She could hear Julie's boots tromp up the stairs and across the hardwood floor. Drawers banged open and closed.

Sheila looked around the living room. Everything

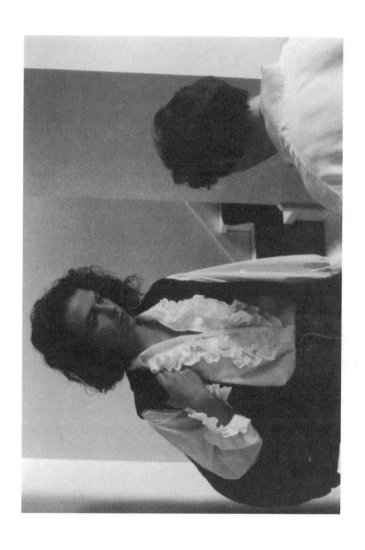

in it whispered of their life together, and held not just memory, but promise. A promise they'd both built their futures on. But she now knew that there had been a crack in their foundation from the start. Something missing, broken, unanswered. Maybe she'd always known that, just quashed its implications. Yes, that was the truth. She had always known it. Marked, in fact, the very passage of her life using the milestones of Lynn's presence and absence.

What, then, of her immense and uncomplicated love for Julie? And her fundamental belief in the supremacy of loyalty? No paradigm accounted for the workings of her heart. It was beyond intellect. Beyond humor. Beyond her.

She found herself at the foot of the stairs. She heard the zip of a bag, then footsteps approaching. She pulled her shirt up to her face and wiped the streaming tears.

Julie appeared on the landing and stopped when she saw Sheila. "Talk to me when you know." She hiked her duffel bag over her shoulder, brushed past Sheila and out the front door.

Sheila cringed at the slam. Turned her face away. Caught the scent of Lynn on her shirt.

Lynn gripped the banister and dragged herself up the lobby stairs, toward the elevators. She was exhausted and wanted nothing more than a scalding shower, cool sheets. She pushed the button for the elevator, waited, pushed it again. She looked around. The restaurant wasn't crowded yet. Maybe she'd order a cup of tea and have it sent up to the room.

She tracked a waiter with her eyes, then spotted Bill sitting alone against the windows, staring at her. She almost didn't recognize him. He never wore T-shirts in public. His face looked dark and unshaved, his short hair wavy and unbrushed.

Bill's gaze stayed locked on Lynn as she approached, but she could not read his expression. After fourteen years, she was seeing an entirely new face. She gestured toward the empty chair. He nodded for her to sit down. A menu was handed over her shoulder from behind. She pushed it back without turning around. "Just tea, please. No, make it coffee."

Bill rolled the pepper shaker between his palms. When he spoke, his tone was measured. "I spent all of last night looking all over town for you. I can only guess how *you* spent the night."

"It's not what you think." She couldn't stop a small chuckle. "Believe me."

Bill was unamused. "Well then, enlighten me."

The waiter returned with coffee and filled Lynn's cup. Bill's was still full. Untouched, like his breakfast. "Anything wrong, sir?"

"Everything's fine." Bill kept his eyes on Lynn, who was growing nauseous at the sight of rubbery beige eggs and grease-hardened bacon.

"Can I take that away for you?" The waiter reached for the plate.

Bill blocked his hand. "No." He turned back to Lynn. "I think I'll keep it."

"Very well, sir."

Lynn diverted her eyes to the red napkin-fan lodged in her water glass. She removed it, unfolded it and flattened it against her lap.

Once the waiter was out of earshot, Bill pushed his plate aside and folded his hands on the table. "So . . . ?"

Lynn sipped her coffee, touched her napkin to her lips. "I was with Sheila."

Bill leaned back in his chair, stared up at the ceiling. "Here it comes . . ."

"Look, there's something you don't know . . ." There were many things he didn't know. Lynn had wanted it that way. He didn't know that there hadn't been any other men since they'd been married. She'd let him think there were, in some freakish attempt at self-protection. He didn't know that although there'd been no women either, that was all she'd ever wanted. And he didn't know that almost no night passed without her dreaming of Sheila while sleeping by his side.

Lynn sipped her coffee and studied Bill across the table. Although she'd never been in love with him, she had loved him. She still did, and she dreaded the hand she would have in his undoing. "Sheila and I . . . we know each other from a long time ago."

How big was the lie? Bill wasn't sure he wanted to know. "You've been maneuvering for two years to get this show produced, and you neglect to tell me that you and Sheila used to be friends? I can't even . . ."

"We were more than friends . . ."

Bill glanced around quickly to see if anyone was listening. He leaned forward. "How much more?"

An aspiring caffeine buzz only accented Lynn's exhaustion. Her eyes wanted to be closed. "Look . . . can we talk about this in the morning?"

"It IS morning!"

"Oh, yeah . . ." her voice trailed off. She stood and looked at Bill. "Please excuse me." She headed for the elevators.

Bill threw his napkin on his plate and took off after her.

"Why didn't you talk to me about this?" Bill paced the room like a caged animal, vacillating between fight and flight.

Lynn sat at the edge of the bed and followed Bill with her eyes. "I felt like I had to deal with it on my own." Partly true, but what she really wanted to say was "I'm sorry." Sorry for promising an impossibility . . . sorry for delaying the inevitable.

Bill stared out at the waking city. The mountains carved a gray ridge across the crisp blue horizon, looking somehow two-dimensional. A breeze drew the evergreens into a shimmering wave that rolled across the park below. Boats rocked in their slips along the marina. Bill wished he was down by the water, barefoot, jeans cuffed up, sharing a loaf of pumpernickel with the gulls. Or even back at the office, three meetings in progress and six calls on hold. Anywhere but in this room, in this conversation.

He tugged at the back of his hair and rubbed the scratch of his unshaved face. "I thought we were together. A couple, you know?" He turned to Lynn. "When things come up, you work them out."

Lynn wasn't sure how to have this discussion, what direction to take it. She was short on explanations when it came to this part of herself, but she knew there was no turning back. It had taken too long and been too painful. "This isn't something you can 'work out.' "

Lynn's declaration caught Bill totally off guard.

Forceful and final, it left him no room to propose the recommendations he'd prepared, no venue for the performance he'd rehearsed ... He stormed to the desk, grabbed Sheila's contract from Lynn's briefcase, and waved it at her. "I wish she'd never come into the picture." He pulled the trash can from under the desk and threw the contract in. "Goddammit!" His foot connected successfully, sending the can spiraling across the room. It cracked against the wall behind Lynn, splintering into plastic shards.

"It's not that simple," Lynn yelled. "This isn't about Sheila, it's about *me.*"

"Just fucking great ..." Bill's contempt was palpable. "My wife's a dyke!" He couldn't bear to look at her — could barely survive the images running through his own mind. He turned away, then saw the sculpture on the glass shelf.

Realizing what was about to happen, Lynn lunged toward him. "NO!"

Then came the crash ... a rain of glass and shattered body parts — another memory made that would forever beg to be exorcised. Typically, after an exchange of *mea culpa,* they'd make polite amends in bed. A not uncommon phenomenon, yet somehow curious and uneasy for these two people who'd grown so far from love. But bed could no longer be a part of their vernacular, and they had little else to work with.

They eyed each other suspiciously, then retreated to their corners as their unarticulated pact demanded. Lynn dialed housekeeping to come clean up the mess, then locked herself in the bathroom for a two-hour mineral soak. Bill turned on "Lifestyles of the Rich

142

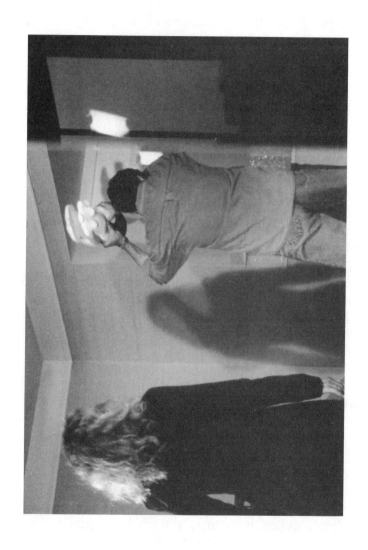

and Famous." Disappointed by a rerun, he soon fell asleep in his chair, and dreamt of a would-be king trapped in the upper echelons of mediocrity.

♥ ♥ ♥

Stella barked wildly as the doorbell rang again and again. There was a pause, then some noise around back. She bolted through the living room and jumped against the sliding glass doors.

"Sheila!" Katie knocked on the glass and peered into the unlit room. "Sheila!" She backed away from the house, yelled up toward the bedroom. "SHEILA!"

"Why are you yelling..." Competing with the strong wind, Sheila's voice echoed faintly from the shoreline.

Though the night was moonless, Katie knew where to find Sheila. She trudged across the dark beach and down the length of the dock. Sheila was curled on the floor of the rowboat. Katie looked down at her. "Get up!"

Sheila half-opened her eyes. "Why?"

Katie shoved the boat with her foot. "Get up!"

Sheila struggled to prop herself up but couldn't find the energy. She dropped back into the boat.

"Your show starts in less than an hour!"

"I feel sick." Sheila pulled her knees up against her chest. "I just wanna sleep." She felt disoriented and slightly nauseous from a day spent drifting in and out of sleep on choppy waters.

"Listen to me!" Katie bent down, grabbed hold of the boat, pulled it against the dock. "I just talked to Bill. He thinks he made a mistake offering you the show, and I had to do some fast talking to convince him he was wrong. He'll be there tonight, and I promised him *you'd* change his mind."

Sheila looked up at Katie. "Lynn kissed me."

"Jesus Christ. Sheila..." Katie's heart ached at the realization she could no longer play the role of Sheila's friend. She felt a sense of personal betrayal that enraged her. "Look, if you want to fuck up your personal life, that's your business, but this is *WORK*, and that's *MY* business. Now, *GET UP!*"

The small boat rocked as Sheila struggled to her feet and hauled herself onto the dock. "You wouldn't understand."

Katie's red hair blew madly in the wind, slapping across her pale cheeks. "Don't you even try that with me." Her tone was cold. "I understand. And I think it stinks."

Sheila felt exposed, chilled by the mix of Katie's words and the cool night air. She tucked her hands under her sweatshirt, turned and started back toward the house. She listened for a call from Katie, imagined being tackled to the ground from behind... part of her wanting so much to be stopped, held, given Katie's blessing.

Katie stood firm. She couldn't believe Sheila was walking away. It went against her Aries nature, which typically compelled a digging in of heels, the mounting of a massive defense. Sheila's flight revealed conflict, self-doubt — perhaps there was still time to tip the scales. "In case you're interested," she called out after her, "Julie's at my place."

Sheila dropped her clothes to the floor and

stepped into the shower. She knew she had to rush to get to the club on time. Her future seemed to be riding on tonight's show. But she felt weak and thoroughly exhausted, and when the memories once again began to overtake her, she did not put up a fight . . . and slipped slowly into the past.

Twenty years old again . . . huddled in the corner of her apartment . . . caged by a semi-circle of photographs. Her clothes are rain-soaked and stick to her skin. She is trembling, chilled, confused. Is it still her birthday? Was that scene with Lynn just hours ago? The photos come to life around her. Captured moments springing free of their Polaroid prosceniums, dancing in the third dimension. The fool and her queen of hearts enacting the bewildering spectacle of love's last desperate breaths. A convoluted passion play. The merging of joy and suffering until they are indistinguishable and one. She knows she is going crazy and doesn't care. She invites it, slides down its slippery slope. Does not look away when Lynn's eyes surround her . . . lots of them, everywhere, piercing and penetrating. Lynn's laugh fills the room, relentless, inescapable, beckoning like a siren . . . "Come, maroon yourself on me . . ."

She rips a match from its pack, ignites it, slowly feeds a photograph to the hungry flame. Emulsion sizzles across the surface, distorting the image. When it burns her hand she tosses it down and draws another. An act of self-defense. The viewfinder dangles from her fingertips like a tiny rosary . . . a single relic spared from the pyre. She tries to remember childhood prayers but cannot. She stares into space, catatonic, as fire blazes across the shag carpet and licks the curtains edge . . .

146

Sheila found herself crouched on the floor of the shower. Water shot down at her like needles. She squeezed her face between her hands, wiped back her hair. Had she missed her show? Her skin felt cold from the tile and scalded from the thick steam. Using the plastic curtain to steady herself, she feebly rose to her feet, shut off the water and reached for a towel.

Sheila squinted her eyes and stared into a swirling cloud of blue and red smoke. The microphone buzzed with feedback as she twisted it from its stand. The spotlight glared down on her. She heard muffled cheers that grew distant and faded into silence.

Katie felt panic. Sheila's clothes were rumpled and her eyes seemed glazed over. Angry as Katie was, she didn't want to watch Sheila crash and burn on stage. She looked across the table at Bill. Could he tell something was wrong? How much did he know about what was going on? For that matter, how much did *she* even know? More than she really wanted to.

The room was dead quiet. Lynn couldn't see Sheila well from the back of the club, but the long silence made her uneasy. She wanted the show to be over so they could talk. She needed to tell Sheila that she'd come clean with Bill. That she was free now. Free to give Sheila what she'd wanted all this time. What they'd both wanted all this time.

A lone fan hooted in excitement. Several people clapped. Sheila cleared her throat. "Let's talk about old flames." Her voice was barely audible. "Old flames . . ." She stared up into the lights. The audience dissolved into a red-orange-blue blur. Slipping . . .

A loud bang. The door crashes open, swings back into the wall. Something yellow comes at her through the flames. Boots. A strange mask. A shoulder punches into her ribs, knocking the breath out of her. She's being lifted. Everything is spinning . . . now upside down. The carpet glides by . . . the viewfinder dangles from her thumb. She feels cool air and hears sirens.

"Hey Sheeeeila . . . Where arrrre youuuu?" Uneasy laughter spread through the room, and Katie was filled with dread.

"I'm sorry . . ." Sheila slid the microphone back into its stand. "This isn't funny anymore."

Heads turned and voices murmured as Sheila walked offstage. Katie had no words to stop Bill as he stood, shook her hand, and left the club. She charged through the crowd toward the dressing room.

She pushed the door closed behind her, leaned against it and faced Sheila's back. Her rage was quiet, focused like a laser. "What the hell is the matter with you?"

Sheila watched Katie in the mirror. How could she explain that her entire career had been built on a tragedy? All the jokes about unrequited love, coming out, relationships gone bad, years of therapy. It was all colorful wrapping for her own devastation. And even though humor *was* a high-level defense mechanism, she was feeling drained and not very defensive anymore. She didn't think she could keep pulling it off, and wasn't sure she wanted to. "I'm the butt of my own jokes." She reconsidered, shook her head. "I AM the joke."

"I couldn't have said that better." Katie's tone was biting.

Sheila spun around on her stool and caught the last semblance of respect dropping from Katie's eyes. She felt utterly alone.

Katie knew Sheila was in pain, but had to speak the truth about what she saw. Honesty had always been an unspoken commitment between them, and there had never been more on the line than right now. "This fantasy you're playing out comes with a high price tag."

The words hit their target and stung. Over the years, Sheila had grown to rely on Katie as a barometer of her own integrity; a singular tribunal on the correctness of her path. And Katie's feedback had been unfailingly sound . . . inevitably resonating with what Sheila herself already knew. But, for the first time, Sheila felt Katie didn't understand. Perhaps she'd never told Katie enough to make her realize that she and Lynn should have been together all along. It had just taken them a lifetime to grow perfect for each other. "I've waited too long for this . . ."

Katie grieved this confirmation of what she'd feared most. Her child was losing a godparent, Julie was losing a lover, she was losing her best friend. Their family, so long in the making, had been decimated in an instant. "I've been up and down with you, Sheila . . ." Katie fought to break from Sheila's pleading stare. "But I can't go where you're going now."

Closing the door behind her was the hardest thing Katie ever had to do. Sheila knew that, and did not try to stop her. And then she quickly got to thinking that if Katie had been a real friend, she wouldn't be walking out. She'd support her no matter what. She was obviously taking Julie's side, who she hadn't even *known* as long . . .

And right before Sheila got to the "Who needs her anyway?" part, she realized she didn't believe any of it. Katie's friendship was not in question. But neither was her own love for Lynn. How could it be, after years of being held sacrosanct, fueled by a potent mix of desire and imagination. For a moment, she wondered if that might really be all there was to it — desire and imagination — but then Lynn appeared at the door, and not a single thing but her seemed real.

Bluish street light slipped through the Levolors, dividing Julie's face into bands of light and shadow. The house was dark, except for a solitary red candle that dripped down itself and puddled onto the glass table, layering wax stalactites along its path of descent. Although Katie had nearly two hundred CD's, Julie couldn't find a thing she'd wanted to listen to. Everything was too depressing, or too upbeat, or too something else. So she spent the evening in silence and darkness. She wondered how the show was going, whether Sheila would be seeing Lynn again tonight, whether her life was about to change for good. It was already unrecognizable.

Katie came into the house from the back,

thinking Julie must be sleeping because all the lights were off. As she came around the corner into the living room, she saw Julie standing by the window. An unfamiliar Julie, somehow devitalized, looking like a kid stuck outside a playground fence or hustled past a toy store window. Wanting. The type of wanting that adults, wearing their bruises as badges, typically come to consider a liability and promptly abandon.

Julie must have sensed Katie's presence, because she turned and looked at her. A question hung in the air between them. It was asked and answered without a word. Julie had always been able to read more in a face than most people could hear in an explanation. There was an openness about her that, paradoxical in the way all truths are, accounted for both her sensitivity and her strength. But Katie watched yet another domino prepare to fall, as Julie teetered on the edge of shutting down . . . in the name of growing up.

Lynn could feel Bill's stare as she folded her clothes into the suitcase. It had been hours since the last word was spoken between them, and the conversation loomed too big to know where to start again. So they busied themselves with other things, just like they did at home — each with their individualized way of adding bricks to the wall between them. They wanted to talk, but it was as if that capacity had somehow been bred out of the species from which they'd both descended. It was a mystery to them how two people with their level of intelligence and professional achievement could not know how to have a conversation with each other that had a beginning, middle and end. Of course, if they could have done that, they probably never would have married.

But they did — the blind leading the blind down the aisle, struggling in darkness until sometime around their sixth year together when they really just stopped trying. It wasn't a conscious decision, but something changed and they both knew it. At first they both felt relief, but soon they realized it was resignation in disguise. And that sparked discontent, which fueled resentment and further withdrawal.

And against this backdrop, Lynn had lived a secret life, mostly in her own mind. So many nights, springing awake from dreams of women's hands on her body. In a sweaty panic, trying to slip out of bed without tugging the sheets in the way that always woke Bill. Running to the shower, scraping herself with soap, masturbating . . .

And, all the while, Bill decorated his office with bright, attractive women . . . even though he noticed them as little as he did the constant redecorations of his own home. And he drove past the hookers on some nights, but never picked one up . . . knowing he'd only end up thinking of Lynn and wishing he was with her. Perhaps he should have left the marriage early on, but he never wanted to. He just wanted things to be different, and he didn't know what to do about it.

And then one night, several years ago, he'd had a dream that felt not of his own making — like it had drifted into his mind as a whole from somewhere else — and he'd sat up the rest of the night watching Lynn sleep, desperate to conjure some image to oppose the one his unconscious had just betrayed him with. But by morning he knew the truth.

He watched Lynn now, folding the silk robe he'd given her, laying it in her suitcase. It suddenly seemed real to him that she was leaving, but for some reason he wanted to hear her say it. He lit a cigarette, took a drag, tried to sound casual. "You don't usually pack until morning..."

Lynn stacked several shirts and did not look at him. "I need to be with Sheila."

Having heard it, he felt even worse. Why had he walked right into that? He crossed past Lynn and stepped out onto the terrace. Twenty-three floors down to Bayside Street... and for a moment, he imagined falling through the night air.

Lynn zipped her suitcase shut. "What, no argument?"

"Look..." Bill turned to Lynn. She looked tired and scared. Suddenly it didn't seem so hard to talk. He knew exactly what he had to say. "I've seen this coming for a long time. I'm sorry about this afternoon." He shook his head. "I just wasn't ready to know for sure."

Lynn didn't quite know how to respond. It had been so long since they'd spoken honestly. It reminded her of when they were first together. It reminded her how much she loved him. And she was filled with an awareness of how much her silence had hurt him. She set her suitcase on the floor, joined him on the terrace. "Can I... have a cigarette?"

Bill smiled weakly. "I thought you quit smoking..."

Lynn watched a ferry wrap around Lion's Point and disappear behind the mountain. "Quitting smoking is a complicated thing." Her words bore the cumbrous weight of deeper, unarticulated meaning.

Bill pulled a cigarette from his pocket, lit it and handed it to Lynn. She took a drag, then looked him in the eye. "Thank you." She took his face in her hands, spoke from a place inside herself she'd forgotten until that moment. "Thank you . . ."

Bill's eyes filled with tears and Lynn embraced him. They held each other for a long while and though they were silent, everything passed between them . . . and then was let go.

Although the breeze hummed through the chimes, and the tide splashed against the dock on its way up the beach, the night seemed incredibly quiet, and the house seemed incredibly empty. Sheila sorted through jeans and polo shirts, pulled socks and underwear from drawers, slipped favorite jackets off hangers. Stella waited patiently on the bed, hoping the suitcase would soon be moved from her favorite sleeping spot. Sheila interpreted the watchful stare as a guilt trip, and tried to disregard the sentiment that this departure was different than any other.

Stella's ears perked up, and there was a knock at the door. Sheila glanced at herself in the mirror, pushed her bangs out of her eyes and slipped Doc Martens over her bare feet. Although she'd been expecting Lynn, it was strange to see her standing in the doorway, to invite her in, to know that she'd be spending the night. Sheila wished they were somewhere else, somewhere neutral, somewhere *not* the home she'd made with Julie. But the night would soon be over, and in the morning they would leave together.

As Lynn wearily dragged her luggage and herself into the house, Sheila felt an extraordinary sense that one chapter had come to an end, and another was beginning.

♥ ♥ ♥

Julie ran her thumbs across the belly of the small clay form. She shaped shoulder blades, fashioned a familiar face, then squished it back into a cold, wet ball. She'd been doing the same thing for hours, trapped in a trance-like withdrawal. Katie had offered to stay up with her, but there was really no point. It was going to be a long night, and she wanted to be as alone as she felt.

She curled herself under a sheet on the sofa and stared at the ceiling. Everything about herself and her relationship with Sheila was now thrown into question. Had it all been a big lie? Had Lynn been party to their entire relationship, her memory steering them relentlessly off-track like a wobbly third wheel? Was Lynn the inaccessible destination that kept Sheila's suitcase always packed? The skin that Sheila felt through? The shadow in their bed?

Nothing could be more awful, more completely devastating, than the thought that all these years Sheila had loved someone else. Julie felt the sting of being "second choice." A stand-in — convenient and available — and now, replaceable. Tears ran sideways down her face and dripped onto the red leather. Only

their cadence marked time, and the night seemed never-ending.

♥ ♥ ♥

Sheila reached under the bed, felt around for her Boris and Natasha slippers, knew what the smooth stone was as soon as her fingers touched it. Julie's tourmaline earring, lost since the night they'd worked themselves into a sweat on the floor by the fireplace. They'd joked that it would turn up again next time they made love on the floor. Anyway, Julie would be glad to get it back . . .

A breeze filled the living room with the scent of freesia as Lynn slid the glass door open and let Stella out onto the back deck. She had already canvassed the room for things to do while Sheila packed upstairs. She'd searched the CD collection for anything familiar, leafed through several metaphysically-titled hardbacks, smoked half a pack of Benson and Hedges . . . but the surroundings felt alien and refused to welcome her. She switched off the light, laid down on the couch, stared at the band that hadn't left her finger for fourteen years. Amazing, that a whole woman could hide behind twelve grams of gold that made only the faintest clink when dropped into the ashtray.

Sheila placed the tourmaline earring on the night table, knowing Julie would find it there when . . . when she came to pack her stuff, or whatever. She noticed the framed photograph of the two of them, pulled it towards her, picked it up. Katie's words played in her mind. "At the rate you're going, you'll soon be having that same 'perfect' relationship with a photograph of Julie . . ."

"Hard to be committed, easy to get committed," she joked to herself, but it didn't seem funny. Where was the humor in this situation? Just one tiny, little island to stand on and laugh.

On impulse, she stuck the picture in her suitcase. Maybe she'd take the earring too. After all, she hadn't stopped loving Julie. A week ago she believed they'd be spending the rest of their lives together . . .

But even a week ago, she and Julie weren't alone. Lynn had always been there between them, haunting their relationship in ways Sheila seldom recognized and never acknowledged. And now the ghost had come to life. An unexpected resurrection, forcing an unimaginable reckoning.

Sheila knelt before her dresser, slid open the bottom drawer, removed the cherrywood box — a microcosm of the irony that was her life. Her personal Pandora's Box, filled with cards, photographs, souvenirs, tokens of her life with Julie. And in their midst, the viewfinder . . . reigning like a silent despot. She'd paid it secret visits through the years, feeling foolish and guilty and like she'd never grown up. But, simply, it was a measure of her devotion to Lynn. And, surely, *that* was beyond question or reproach.

To weigh love against love seemed absurd at best — calamitous at worst. Yet the geometry of a triangle would never lend itself toward resolution, and to endeavor down one path while moored to another would certainly doom the journey. If nothing else, Sheila knew this painful explosion of her life was a lesson in letting go. And therein lay the question she had yet to put to herself.

She took the viewfinder from the box, held it to her eye, and saw the familiar smiles of two people intoxicated by each other's presence. She thought back to the moment Lynn first walked into the conference room, clearly remembering that beneath the shock, the fear, the anger, their ancient connection had still pulsed. Present and potent. Manifested in the flesh. And the question now before her, the challenge she faced, was not who to love — she loved them both — but who to let go.

She removed the framed photograph from her suitcase, stared at Julie's image and felt an overwhelming pull tinged with sadness. She could no longer wrap her mind around the possibility of being with Julie, feeling the way she did about Lynn. It didn't seem fair. Perhaps it never had been.

She slid the photograph into the memento box and closed the lid.

Lynn looked almost fragile, curled like a child on the couch, blonde hair wrapped across her cheeks, her eyes. It had been a long time since Sheila had watched Lynn sleep. When they were young, Sheila would roll to the far side of the bed and pretend to doze off, then rebel against her own exhaustion until Lynn's breathing slowed to its familiar rhythm — the rhythm her chest now rose and fell to in the dim, golden glow of moonlight.

She could remember it as if no time had passed.

She'd grumble sleep noises, slide Lynn's way, stretch a foot or elbow to touch her skin. Every nerve in her body at attention, every inch of her aching to be covered by every inch of Lynn.

And on those rare occasions when she could fall asleep at all, her sleep was fitful, permeated by the fear she might awake to find herself wrapped around Lynn. Her terrifying, exhilarating secret exposed.

And wondering — only half-wondering really, because part of her knew it must be true — if sometimes Lynn didn't lay awake watching her too.

She rolled the viewfinder between her palms, tempted to rouse Lynn and show her the salvaged treasure, to share a laugh and confirm they were meant to be together. The proof was in her hands.

But instead, she pulled a quilt from the closet and laid it gently over Lynn's slender frame. She placed the viewfinder on the glass table, noticed the gold band in the ashtray, and suddenly grasped the stunning reality that Lynn was fully and finally hers.

Sheila latched the suitcase shut. The bedroom felt cool, but her shirt clung to her body, damp with a strange sweat. She pulled the glass door open and stepped out onto the porch. The moon seemed a sliver of smile in the sky. Was it laughing with her or at her . . . ? For a moment, she expected Julie's hands to slide around her from behind, pull her close, like they'd done so many times before. And then she remembered. And Julie's absence felt like a huge hole through which her own soul leaked into the night.

She wandered into the dark blue quiet of Julie's

studio, searching for elusive answers she held no hope of finding. Encircled by bold, animated paintings, smooth, sensuous sculptures, mad mixtures of collage — the moody junctures of Julie's experimentation, steeped now in a sadness not their own.

The easel stood in the corner like a solitary monument, covered by a paint-splattered sheet. A work-in-progress — to have been presented on her upcoming birthday, just days away. She approached the gift slowly, with the reverence she'd always felt toward Julie's work. She tugged the sheet gently, tentatively, till it dropped to the floor.

Tears welled in her eyes, as she stared at the image confronting her. Poignant and compelling... and desecrated. The faces, clearly her own and Julie's, were locked in a gaze which spoke volumes about the connection between them. But Julie's dark, brown curls had been painted over with wild, tormented strokes of golden-yellow, creating a blonde mane. Lynn's hair ... Julie's face ... Lynn's hair ...

Sheila pounded her fists against her forehead, covered her eyes, swallowed back the eruption bursting through her belly and chest ... then forced herself to look again. She faced the irrefutable evidence of her lover's agony, and the raw imprint of her own betrayal ...

She stumbled backward and collapsed into a chair. Alone with the clamor of her conscience, with no incoming judgments to defend against, Sheila glimpsed beyond the sacredness of her tie to Lynn and into its barest nature. Its power, equally enchanting and insidious, had permeated not only her relationship with Julie, but all the fragile links she'd

162

tried to establish over the years. Did she dare still think of it as love? It had deep roots in love, but had grown like wild weeds into a tangled bower that surrounded her entirely. And if she could loosen its grip, choose freely to love, what choice would she make? Whose hand would she take?

She laid her head against the drafting table, buried her face in her arms, and succumbed to a fatigue that pulled her down into the depths of sleep.

Dreams came rapidly. Fragments of images approached, transformed, receded. And then the familiar voice called from the woods, and this time Sheila did not hesitate. She stepped into the mossy forest bed without looking back and hastened through the snarled ferns, toward the open field. She called to Lynn, who danced among the rows of moonlit sunflowers, and raced into her tight embrace, safe and all-encompassing. Laughter echoed the joy of their union. And as the dirt drew her down into its cool body, this time she did not acquiesce . . . did not sink gently into its darkness. Instead, she struggled toward a light whose intensity grew with each kick and thrust and scream she released — until she stood sovereign and fully illuminated.

The car horn startled Sheila, ripping her from a long dream she could barely remember. Morning light bathed the studio. Chimes tinkled in the wind. She looked around the room, still awakening by degrees. Julie's face . . . Lynn's hair . . . The car horn beckoned again.

Lynn waited by the front door and smiled sleepily as Sheila descended the steps. At last they were on their way, and things would be set right. Their future was too new to imagine, but Lynn had forfeited everything for this moment. When Sheila hesitated on the landing, Lynn quickly picked up both of their suitcases and headed out the door . . .

.

listening for the sound of Sheila's footsteps behind her.

Sheila stepped outside and inhaled the morning mist. A plane crossed overhead and disappeared behind the mountains. She tried to imagine herself on it, traveling south to begin a new life. She pulled the front door closed behind her, and began what felt like a long walk up the path to the carport.

The taxi driver was loading Lynn's bag into the trunk as Sheila came around the side of the car. Though not typically attuned to such things, he sensed a strange energy in the air that left him uneasy. "Beautiful day today . . ." He forced a chuckle. The women stared at each other, silent. It was going to be a long ride to the airport. He bent to lift Sheila's suitcase, and was surprised when her hand reached down and held it firmly in place. He stood and looked at her, uncertain what to do. Her eyes were locked on Lynn. He closed the trunk. "I'll just . . . wait . . . in the car." He motioned to the cab, then hurried around the side and got in.

Sheila watched as Lynn's expression evolved from confusion to the painful recognition that Sheila was not going with her.

"Sheila . . ." Lynn's eyes filled with tears. Sheila stepped forward and embraced her. An immense flow of feeling passed between them, which Sheila could now indeed, with confidence and clarity, define as love. But it was a love for something they'd shared a long time ago. A love of what they'd meant to each other, given to each other, learned from each other. A love that had tried to contort itself into everything other than what it really had been and was meant to be — the most precious and influential friendship of both their lives.

As they relinquished their embrace, Sheila opened her mouth to speak, but Lynn raised her hand and gently pressed her fingers against Sheila's lips. There was nothing she needed to hear — no apology, no consolation. She'd known since the night of the party that Sheila and Julie were truly in love, and had only hoped to somehow draw Sheila back into her life. But now she understood that although Sheila had served as a catalyst for her self-realization, she was not meant to travel that path with her. And though the thought would take some getting used to, she knew there would be other women in her future — and maybe one day, she'd even find a love like the one so clearly captured in the photograph she'd seen on Sheila's night table.

She squeezed Sheila's hands, so soft and familiar, then let them drop and backed away.

Sheila moved her suitcase from behind the cab and watched Lynn slide into the back seat and pull the door closed. Her stomach tied itself in knots, as the driver started the engine and pulled into the street. But somehow, she knew their friendship would endure . . . and Lynn's trembling smile revealed she knew it too. By the time the cab disappeared around the corner, Sheila's mind was already racing on to other things.

The rowboat creaked, tugging against its ropes as the tide pulled back from the shore. The morning was crisp and clear, the sky a blue more vivid than Sheila had seen in a long time. She unlooped the ropes from the piling and pulled the boat against the dock. It had served her well, and felt like an old friend. She ran her hand along its worn surface, knocked twice on the bow, pointed it toward the sea. With a push of her foot, the small craft merged with the outgoing tide, and slowly pulled away.

Linden was surprised to see Sheila hop over the fence into the goat pen. It wasn't her day to work — the donkey had already been put out to pasture — but he could tell by her determined gait that she had something on her mind. She looked somehow different, and though he couldn't put his finger on it, it was definitely something good. She gave him a big hug, shared a curious tale, and proposed a deal that he gladly closed with a handshake.

♥ ♥ ♥

Katie balanced herself on top of the back stairs, leaned over the landing, and hammered a nail into the side of the house. South side, where the sun lounged most of the day. A row of clay pots would soon be hanging, filled with earth and sprouting her favorite herbs. She heard a strange, guttural cry — like braying — which, of course, would be impossible. She twisted her head and looked down into the back yard.

"I have a Snow White complex!" Sheila announced proudly, perched bareback on the white donkey, arms outstretched. Princely, charming and irresistible.

Katie smiled, despite herself. She was still angry, hurt, and disappointed — but most of all, she was relieved that her dream last night had been accurate, in outcome, if not detail. She shook her head. "You're an ass!"

Sheila leaned forward and covered the donkey's ears. "Awww, don't listen to her."

Katie studied Sheila but remained silent.

Sheila sobered. "I'm sorry about the show. I have to get there some other way, on my own."

Katie turned and craned her neck in through the back door. "Julie! I think you should come out here!"

Sheila steered the donkey across the yard to the bottom of the steps. Julie watched from the landing. She knew the display was a gesture to win her back, but she wasn't ready to be won back just yet.

Sheila slid off the donkey and climbed several steps. She looked up at the four eyes that stared down at her. "Please ... excuse us ... ," she stuttered to Katie.

Katie squeezed Julie's hand, then disappeared into the house. Julie leaned back against the door. Sheila climbed a few steps closer. "I was just in the neighborhood and ... I thought I'd trot by!" She grinned sheepishly.

Julie was unmoved. This hook was too big for Sheila to get off of with a joke.

Sheila shuffled around. "You said I should talk to you when I know ..." She wanted to reach for Julie, to feel her touch ... Instead she looked her in the eye and spoke softly. "I know." The words sent a sensation through her whole body. She really did know. For the first time, she really *knew*. "I love you ..."

Julie could feel Sheila's longing to hold her. And

as she descended toward her, there was no one in the way. The path was clear. The ghost was gone.

"I even unpacked..." Sheila grinned. "Everything!"

Sheila was back... or maybe there for the first time. Julie laughed, raised her palm perpendicular to her face. Sheila completed their ritual, poking two fingers toward Julie's tear-filled eyes.

"Your pumpkin is leaving..." Julie motioned toward the yard.

Sheila turned and saw the donkey munching his way across the grass, toward the back alley. "That was Cinderella..." Sheila chuckled. "This is a different story."

Julie caressed Sheila's face and looked straight into her eyes, then knocked their foreheads together playfully. "You shit!"

Sheila smiled and pulled her close. They held each other tightly and for a long, long while.

♥ ♥ ♥

Sheila led the donkey down the long expanse of warm sand. Julie rode on its back, watching the dropping sun spill color across the bay. "Sheila..."

Sheila turned slowly, filled with the romance of the moment. "Yes, Julie?"

Julie smiled sweetly, leaned toward her. "My butt hurts!"

They shared a laugh, a long deep kiss, and continued on their way.

A few of the publications of
THE NAIAD PRESS, INC.
P.O. Box 10543 • Tallahassee, Florida 32302
Phone (904) 539-5965
Toll-Free Order Number: 1-800-533-1973
Mail orders welcome. Please include 15% postage.

FOR LOVE AND FOR LIFE: INTIMATE PORTRAITS OF
LESBIAN COUPLES by Susan Johnson. 224 pp.
ISBN 1-56280-091-4 $14.95

DEVOTION by Mindy Kaplan. 192 pp. See the movie — read
the book!   ISBN 1-56280-093-0   10.95

SOMEONE TO WATCH by Jaye Maiman. 272 pp. A Robin Miller
mystery. 4th in a series.   ISBN 1-56280-095-7   10.95

GREENER THAN GRASS by Jennifer Fulton. 208 pp. A young
woman — a stranger in her bed.   ISBN 1-56280-092-2   10.95

TRAVELS WITH DIANA HUNTER by Regine Sands. Erotic
lesbian romp. Audio Book (2 cassettes) ISBN 1-56280-107-4   16.95

CABIN FEVER by Carol Schmidt. 256 pp. Sizzling suspense
and passion.   ISBN 1-56280-089-1   10.95

THERE WILL BE NO GOODBYES by Laura DeHart Young. 192
pp. Romantic love, strength, and friendship.   ISBN 1-56280-103-1   10.95

FAULTLINE by Sheila Ortiz Taylor. 144 pp. Joyous comic
lesbian novel.   ISBN 1-56280-108-2   9.95

OPEN HOUSE by Pat Welch. 176 pp. P.I. Helen Black's fourth
case.   ISBN 1-56280-102-3   10.95

ONCE MORE WITH FEELING by Peggy J. Herring. 240 pp.
Lighthearted, loving romantic adventure.   ISBN 1-56280-089-2   10.95

FOREVER by Evelyn Kennedy. 224 pp. Passionate romance — love
overcoming all obstacles.   ISBN 1-56280-094-9   10.95

WHISPERS by Kris Bruyer. 176 pp. Romantic ghost story
ISBN 1-56280-082-5   10.95

NIGHT SONGS by Penny Mickelbury. 224 pp. A Gianna
Maglione Mystery. Second in a series.   ISBN 1-56280-097-3   10.95

GETTING TO THE POINT by Teresa Stores. 256 pp. Classic
southern Lesbian novel.   ISBN 1-56280-100-7   10.95

PAINTED MOON by Karin Kallmaker. 224 pp. Delicious
Kallmaker romance.   ISBN 1-56280-075-2   9.95

THE MYSTERIOUS NAIAD edited by Katherine V. Forrest &
Barbara Grier. 320 pp. Love stories by Naiad Press authors.
ISBN 1-56280-074-4   14.95

DAUGHTERS OF A CORAL DAWN by Katherine V. Forrest.
240 pp. Tenth Anniversay Edition.   ISBN 1-56280-104-X   10.95

BODY GUARD by Claire McNab. 208 pp. A Carol Ashton Mystery.
6th in a series.   ISBN 1-56280-073-6   10.95

CACTUS LOVE by Lee Lynch. 192 pp. Stories by the beloved
storyteller.   ISBN 1-56280-071-X   9.95

SECOND GUESS by Rose Beecham. 216 pp. An Amanda Valentine
Mystery. 2nd in a series.   ISBN 1-56280-069-8   9.95

THE SURE THING by Melissa Hartman. 208 pp. L.A. earthquake
romance.   ISBN 1-56280-078-7   9.95

A RAGE OF MAIDENS by Lauren Wright Douglas. 240 pp. A
Caitlin Reece Mystery. 6th in a series.   ISBN 1-56280-068-X   9.95

TRIPLE EXPOSURE by Jackie Calhoun. 224 pp. Romantic drama
involving many characters.   ISBN 1-56280-067-1   9.95

UP, UP AND AWAY by Catherine Ennis. 192 pp. Delightful
romance.   ISBN 1-56280-065-5   9.95

PERSONAL ADS by Robbi Sommers. 176 pp. Sizzling short
stories.   ISBN 1-56280-059-0   9.95

FLASHPOINT by Katherine V. Forrest. 256 pp. Lesbian
blockbuster!   ISBN 1-56280-043-4   22.95

CROSSWORDS by Penny Sumner. 256 pp. 2nd Victoria Cross
Mystery.   ISBN 1-56280-064-7   9.95

SWEET CHERRY WINE by Carol Schmidt. 224 pp. A novel of
suspense.   ISBN 1-56280-063-9   9.95

CERTAIN SMILES by Dorothy Tell. 160 pp. Erotic short stories.
ISBN 1-56280-066-3   9.95

EDITED OUT by Lisa Haddock. 224 pp. 1st Carmen Ramirez
Mystery.   ISBN 1-56280-077-9   9.95

WEDNESDAY NIGHTS by Camarin Grae. 288 pp. Sexy
adventure.   ISBN 1-56280-060-4   10.95

SMOKEY O by Celia Cohen. 176 pp. Relationships on the
playing field.   ISBN 1-56280-057-4   9.95

KATHLEEN O'DONALD by Penny Hayes. 256 pp. Rose and
Kathleen find each other and employment in 1909 NYC.
ISBN 1-56280-070-1   9.95

STAYING HOME by Elisabeth Nonas. 256 pp. Molly and Alix
want a baby . . . or do they?   ISBN 1-56280-076-0   10.95

TRUE LOVE by Jennifer Fulton. 240 pp. Six lesbians searching
for love in all the "right" places.   ISBN 1-56280-035-3   9.95

GARDENIAS WHERE THERE ARE NONE by Molleen Zanger.
176 pp. Why is Melanie inextricably drawn to the old house?
ISBN 1-56280-056-6   9.95

KEEPING SECRETS by Penny Mickelbury. 208 pp. A Gianna
Maglione Mystery. First in a series.   ISBN 1-56280-052-3   9.95

THE ROMANTIC NAIAD edited by Katherine V. Forrest &
Barbara Grier. 336 pp. Love stories by Naiad Press authors.
ISBN 1-56280-054-X   14.95

UNDER MY SKIN by Jaye Maiman. 336 pp. A Robin Miller
mystery. 3rd in a series.   ISBN 1-56280-049-3.   10.95

STAY TOONED by Rhonda Dicksion. 144 pp. Cartoons — 1st
collection since *Lesbian Survival Manual.*   ISBN 1-56280-045-0   9.95

CAR POOL by Karin Kallmaker. 272pp. Lesbians on wheels
and then some!   ISBN 1-56280-048-5   9.95

NOT TELLING MOTHER: STORIES FROM A LIFE by Diane
Salvatore. 176 pp. Her 3rd novel.   ISBN 1-56280-044-2   9.95

GOBLIN MARKET by Lauren Wright Douglas. 240pp. A Caitlin
Reece Mystery. 5th in a series.   ISBN 1-56280-047-7   10.95

LONG GOODBYES by Nikki Baker. 256 pp. A Virginia Kelly
mystery. 3rd in a series.   ISBN 1-56280-042-6   9.95

FRIENDS AND LOVERS by Jackie Calhoun. 224 pp. Mid-western
Lesbian lives and loves.   ISBN 1-56280-041-8   10.95

THE CAT CAME BACK by Hilary Mullins. 208 pp. Highly
praised Lesbian novel.   ISBN 1-56280-040-X   9.95

BEHIND CLOSED DOORS by Robbi Sommers. 192 pp. Hot,
erotic short stories.   ISBN 1-56280-039-6   9.95

CLAIRE OF THE MOON by Nicole Conn. 192 pp. See the
movie — read the book!   ISBN 1-56280-038-8   10.95

SILENT HEART by Claire McNab. 192 pp. Exotic Lesbian
romance.   ISBN 1-56280-036-1   10.95

HAPPY ENDINGS by Kate Brandt. 272 pp. Intimate conversations
with Lesbian authors.   ISBN 1-56280-050-7   10.95

THE SPY IN QUESTION by Amanda Kyle Williams. 256 pp.
4th Madison McGuire.   ISBN 1-56280-037-X   9.95

SAVING GRACE by Jennifer Fulton. 240 pp. Adventure and
romantic entanglement.   ISBN 1-56280-051-5   9.95

THE YEAR SEVEN by Molleen Zanger. 208 pp. Women surviving
in a new world.   ISBN 1-56280-034-5   9.95

CURIOUS WINE by Katherine V. Forrest. 176 pp. Tenth Anniver-
sary Edition. The most popular contemporary Lesbian love story.
ISBN 1-56280-053-1   10.95
   Audio Book (2 cassettes)   ISBN 1-56280-105-8   16.95

CHAUTAUQUA by Catherine Ennis. 192 pp. Exciting, romantic
adventure.   ISBN 1-56280-032-9   9.95

A PROPER BURIAL by Pat Welch. 192 pp. A Helen Black
mystery. 3rd in a series.   ISBN 1-56280-033-7   9.95

SILVERLAKE HEAT: A Novel of Suspense by Carol Schmidt.
240 pp. Rhonda is as hot as Laney's dreams.   ISBN 1-56280-031-0   9.95

LOVE, ZENA BETH by Diane Salvatore. 224 pp. The most talked
about lesbian novel of the nineties!   ISBN 1-56280-030-2   10.95

A DOORYARD FULL OF FLOWERS by Isabel Miller. 160 pp.
Stories incl. 2 sequels to *Patience and Sarah*.   ISBN 1-56280-029-9   9.95

MURDER BY TRADITION by Katherine V. Forrest. 288 pp. A
Kate Delafield Mystery. 4th in a series.   ISBN 1-56280-002-7   9.95

THE EROTIC NAIAD edited by Katherine V. Forrest & Barbara
Grier. 224 pp. Love stories by Naiad Press authors.
                                              ISBN 1-56280-026-4   13.95

DEAD CERTAIN by Claire McNab. 224 pp. A Carol Ashton
mystery. 5th in a series.   ISBN 1-56280-027-2   9.95

CRAZY FOR LOVING by Jaye Maiman. 320 pp. A Robin Miller
mystery. 2nd in a series.   ISBN 1-56280-025-6   9.95

STONEHURST by Barbara Johnson. 176 pp. Passionate regency
romance.   ISBN 1-56280-024-8   9.95

INTRODUCING AMANDA VALENTINE by Rose Beecham.
256 pp. An Amanda Valentine Mystery. First in a series.
                                              ISBN 1-56280-021-3   9.95

UNCERTAIN COMPANIONS by Robbi Sommers. 204 pp.
Steamy, erotic novel.   ISBN 1-56280-017-5   9.95

A TIGER'S HEART by Lauren W. Douglas. 240 pp. A Caitlin
Reece mystery. 4th in a series.   ISBN 1-56280-018-3   9.95

PAPERBACK ROMANCE by Karin Kallmaker. 256 pp. A
delicious romance.   ISBN 1-56280-019-1   9.95

MORTON RIVER VALLEY by Lee Lynch. 304 pp. Lee Lynch
at her best!   ISBN 1-56280-016-7   9.95

THE LAVENDER HOUSE MURDER by Nikki Baker. 224 pp.
A Virginia Kelly Mystery. 2nd in a series.   ISBN 1-56280-012-4   9.95

PASSION BAY by Jennifer Fulton. 224 pp. Passionate romance,
virgin beaches, tropical skies.   ISBN 1-56280-028-0   10.95

STICKS AND STONES by Jackie Calhoun. 208 pp. Contemporary
lesbian lives and loves.   ISBN 1-56280-020-5   9.95
Audio Book (2 cassettes)   ISBN 1-56280-106-6   16.95

DELIA IRONFOOT by Jeane Harris. 192 pp. Adventure for Delia
and Beth in the Utah mountains.   ISBN 1-56280-014-0   9.95

UNDER THE SOUTHERN CROSS by Claire McNab. 192 pp.
Romantic nights Down Under.   ISBN 1-56280-011-6   9.95

GRASSY FLATS by Penny Hayes. 256 pp. Lesbian romance in
the '30s.   ISBN 1-56280-010-8   9.95

A SINGULAR SPY by Amanda K. Williams. 192 pp. 3rd
Madison McGuire.   ISBN 1-56280-008-6   8.95

THE END OF APRIL by Penny Sumner. 240 pp. A Victoria
Cross mystery. First in a series.   ISBN 1-56280-007-8   8.95

HOUSTON TOWN by Deborah Powell. 208 pp. A Hollis
Carpenter mystery.   ISBN 1-56280-006-X   8.95

KISS AND TELL by Robbi Sommers. 192 pp. Scorching stories
by the author of *Pleasures.*   ISBN 1-56280-005-1   10.95

STILL WATERS by Pat Welch. 208 pp. A Helen Black mystery.
2nd in a series.   ISBN 0-941483-97-5   9.95

TO LOVE AGAIN by Evelyn Kennedy. 208 pp. Wildly romantic
love story.   ISBN 0-941483-85-1   9.95

IN THE GAME by Nikki Baker. 192 pp. A Virginia Kelly
mystery. First in a series.   ISBN 1-56280-004-3   9.95

AVALON by Mary Jane Jones. 256 pp. A Lesbian Arthurian
romance.   ISBN 0-941483-96-7   9.95

STRANDED by Camarin Grae. 320 pp. Entertaining, riveting
adventure.   ISBN 0-941483-99-1   9.95

THE DAUGHTERS OF ARTEMIS by Lauren Wright Douglas.
240 pp. A Caitlin Reece mystery. 3rd in a series.
                                          ISBN 0-941483-95-9   9.95

CLEARWATER by Catherine Ennis. 176 pp. Romantic secrets
of a small Louisiana town.   ISBN 0-941483-65-7   8.95

THE HALLELUJAH MURDERS by Dorothy Tell. 176 pp. A
Poppy Dillworth mystery. 2nd in a series.   ISBN 0-941483-88-6   8.95

SECOND CHANCE by Jackie Calhoun. 256 pp. Contemporary
Lesbian lives and loves.   ISBN 0-941483-93-2   9.95

BENEDICTION by Diane Salvatore. 272 pp. Striking, contemporary romantic novel.   ISBN 0-941483-90-8   9.95

BLACK IRIS by Jeane Harris. 192 pp. Caroline's hidden past . . .
                                          ISBN 0-941483-68-1   8.95

TOUCHWOOD by Karin Kallmaker. 240 pp. Loving, May/
December romance.   ISBN 0-941483-76-2   9.95

COP OUT by Claire McNab. 208 pp. A Carol Ashton mystery.
4th in a series.   ISBN 0-941483-84-3   9.95

THE BEVERLY MALIBU by Katherine V. Forrest. 288 pp. A
Kate Delafield Mystery. 3rd in a series.   ISBN 0-941483-48-7   10.95

THAT OLD STUDEBAKER by Lee Lynch. 272 pp. Andy's affair
with Regina and her attachment to her beloved car.
ISBN 0-941483-82-7   9.95

PASSION'S LEGACY by Lori Paige. 224 pp. Sarah is swept into
the arms of Augusta Pym in this delightful historical romance.
ISBN 0-941483-81-9   8.95

THE PROVIDENCE FILE by Amanda Kyle Williams. 256 pp.
Second Madison McGuire   ISBN 0-941483-92-4   8.95

I LEFT MY HEART by Jaye Maiman. 320 pp. A Robin Miller
Mystery. First in a series.   ISBN 0-941483-72-X   9.95

THE PRICE OF SALT by Patricia Highsmith (writing as Claire
Morgan). 288 pp. Classic lesbian novel, first issued in 1952 . . .
acknowledged by its author under her own, very famous, name.
ISBN 1-56280-003-5   9.95

SIDE BY SIDE by Isabel Miller. 256 pp. From beloved author of
Patience and Sarah.   ISBN 0-941483-77-0   9.95

STAYING POWER: LONG TERM LESBIAN COUPLES by
Susan E. Johnson. 352 pp. Joys of coupledom. ISBN 0-941-483-75-4   14.95

SLICK by Camarin Grae. 304 pp. Exotic, erotic adventure.
ISBN 0-941483-74-6   9.95

NINTH LIFE by Lauren Wright Douglas. 256 pp. A Caitlin Reece
mystery. 2nd in a series.   ISBN 0-941483-50-9   8.95

PLAYERS by Robbi Sommers. 192 pp. Sizzling, erotic novel.
ISBN 0-941483-73-8   9.95

MURDER AT RED ROOK RANCH by Dorothy Tell. 224 pp.
A Poppy Dillworth mystery. 1st in a series.   ISBN 0-941483-80-0   8.95

LESBIAN SURVIVAL MANUAL by Rhonda Dicksion. 112 pp.
Cartoons!   ISBN 0-941483-71-1   8.95

A ROOM FULL OF WOMEN by Elisabeth Nonas. 256 pp.
Contemporary Lesbian lives.   ISBN 0-941483-69-X   9.95

THEME FOR DIVERSE INSTRUMENTS by Jane Rule. 208 pp.
Powerful romantic lesbian stories.   ISBN 0-941483-63-0   8.95

CLUB 12 by Amanda Kyle Williams. 288 pp. Espionage thriller
featuring a lesbian agent!   ISBN 0-941483-64-9   8.95

DEATH DOWN UNDER by Claire McNab. 240 pp. A Carol
Ashton mystery. 3rd in a series.   ISBN 0-941483-39-8   9.95

MONTANA FEATHERS by Penny Hayes. 256 pp. Vivian and
Elizabeth find love in frontier Montana.   ISBN 0-941483-61-4   8.95

LIFESTYLES by Jackie Calhoun. 224 pp. Contemporary Lesbian
lives and loves.   ISBN 0-941483-57-6   9.95

WILDERNESS TREK by Dorothy Tell. 192 pp. Six women on
vacation learning ''new'' skills.   ISBN 0-941483-60-6   8.95

MURDER BY THE BOOK by Pat Welch. 256 pp. A Helen Black
Mystery. First in a series.   ISBN 0-941483-59-2   9.95

THERE'S SOMETHING I'VE BEEN MEANING TO TELL YOU
Ed. by Loralee MacPike. 288 pp. Gay men and lesbians coming out
to their children.   ISBN 0-941483-44-4   9.95

LIFTING BELLY by Gertrude Stein. Ed. by Rebecca Mark. 104 pp.
Erotic poetry.   ISBN 0-941483-51-7   10.95

AFTER THE FIRE by Jane Rule. 256 pp. Warm, human novel by
this incomparable author.   ISBN 0-941483-45-2   8.95

THREE WOMEN by March Hastings. 232 pp. Golden oldie. A
triangle among wealthy sophisticates. ISBN 0-941483-43-6   8.95

PLEASURES by Robbi Sommers. 204 pp. Unprecedented
eroticism.   ISBN 0-941483-49-5   8.95

EDGEWISE by Camarin Grae. 372 pp. Spellbinding
adventure.   ISBN 0-941483-19-3   9.95

FATAL REUNION by Claire McNab. 224 pp. A Carol Ashton
mystery. 2nd in a series.   ISBN 0-941483-40-1   8.95

IN EVERY PORT by Karin Kallmaker. 228 pp. Jessica's sexy,
adventuresome travels.   ISBN 0-941483-37-7   9.95

OF LOVE AND GLORY by Evelyn Kennedy. 192 pp. Exciting
WWII romance.   ISBN 0-941483-32-0   8.95

CLICKING STONES by Nancy Tyler Glenn. 288 pp. Love
transcending time.   ISBN 0-941483-31-2   9.95

SOUTH OF THE LINE by Catherine Ennis. 216 pp. Civil War
adventure.   ISBN 0-941483-29-0   8.95

WOMAN PLUS WOMAN by Dolores Klaich. 300 pp. Supurb
Lesbian overview.   ISBN 0-941483-28-2   9.95

THE FINER GRAIN by Denise Ohio. 216 pp. Brilliant young
college lesbian novel.   ISBN 0-941483-11-8   8.95

OCTOBER OBSESSION by Meredith More. Josie's rich, secret
Lesbian life.   ISBN 0-941483-18-5   8.95

BEFORE STONEWALL: THE MAKING OF A GAY AND
LESBIAN COMMUNITY by Andrea Weiss & Greta Schiller.
96 pp., 25 illus.   ISBN 0-941483-20-7   7.95

OSTEN'S BAY by Zenobia N. Vole. 204 pp. Sizzling adventure
romance set on Bonaire.   ISBN 0-941483-15-0   8.95

LESSONS IN MURDER by Claire McNab. 216 pp. A Carol
Ashton mystery. First in a series.   ISBN 0-941483-14-2   9.95

YELLOWTHROAT by Penny Hayes. 240 pp. Margarita, bandit,
kidnaps Julia.   ISBN 0-941483-10-X   8.95

SAPPHISTRY: THE BOOK OF LESBIAN SEXUALITY by
Pat Califia. 3d edition, revised. 208 pp.   ISBN 0-941483-24-X   10.95

CHERISHED LOVE by Evelyn Kennedy. 192 pp. Erotic Lesbian
love story.   ISBN 0-941483-08-8   9.95

THE SECRET IN THE BIRD by Camarin Grae. 312 pp. Striking,
psychological suspense novel.   ISBN 0-941483-05-3   8.95

TO THE LIGHTNING by Catherine Ennis. 208 pp. Romantic
Lesbian 'Robinson Crusoe' adventure.   ISBN 0-941483-06-1   8.95

DREAMS AND SWORDS by Katherine V. Forrest. 192 pp.
Romantic, erotic, imaginative stories.   ISBN 0-941483-03-7   8.95

MEMORY BOARD by Jane Rule. 336 pp. Memorable novel
about an aging Lesbian couple.   ISBN 0-941483-02-9   10.95

THE ALWAYS ANONYMOUS BEAST by Lauren Wright Douglas.
224 pp. A Caitlin Reece mystery. First in a series.
                                          ISBN 0-941483-04-5   8.95

PARENTS MATTER by Ann Muller. 240 pp. Parents' relationships with Lesbian daughters and gay sons.   ISBN 0-930044-91-6   9.95

THE BLACK AND WHITE OF IT by Ann Allen Shockley.
144 pp. Short stories.   ISBN 0-930044-96-7   7.95

SAY JESUS AND COME TO ME by Ann Allen Shockley. 288
pp. Contemporary romance.   ISBN 0-930044-98-3   8.95

MURDER AT THE NIGHTWOOD BAR by Katherine V. Forrest.
240 pp. A Kate Delafield mystery. Second in a series.
                                          ISBN 0-930044-92-4   10.95

WINGED DANCER by Camarin Grae. 228 pp. Erotic Lesbian
adventure story.   ISBN 0-930044-88-6   8.95

PAZ by Camarin Grae. 336 pp. Romantic Lesbian adventurer
with the power to change the world.   ISBN 0-930044-89-4   8.95

SOUL SNATCHER by Camarin Grae. 224 pp. A puzzle, an
adventure, a mystery — Lesbian romance.   ISBN 0-930044-90-8   8.95

THE LOVE OF GOOD WOMEN by Isabel Miller. 224 pp.
Long-awaited new novel by the author of the beloved *Patience
and Sarah.*   ISBN 0-930044-81-9   8.95

THE HOUSE AT PELHAM FALLS by Brenda Weathers. 240
pp. Suspenseful Lesbian ghost story.   ISBN 0-930044-79-7   7.95

HOME IN YOUR HANDS by Lee Lynch. 240 pp. More stories
from the author of *Old Dyke Tales.*   ISBN 0-930044-80-0   7.95

PEMBROKE PARK by Michelle Martin. 256 pp. Derring-do
and daring romance in Regency England.   ISBN 0-930044-77-0   7.95

THE LONG TRAIL by Penny Hayes. 248 pp. Vivid adventures
of two women in love in the old west.   ISBN 0-930044-76-2   8.95

AN EMERGENCE OF GREEN by Katherine V. Forrest. 288
pp. Powerful novel of sexual discovery.   ISBN 0-930044-69-X   9.95

THE LESBIAN PERIODICALS INDEX edited by Claire Potter.
432 pp. Author & subject index.   ISBN 0-930044-74-6   12.95

DESERT OF THE HEART by Jane Rule. 224 pp. A classic;
basis for the movie *Desert Hearts.*   ISBN 0-930044-73-8   10.95

TORCHLIGHT TO VALHALLA by Gale Wilhelm. 128 pp.
Classic novel by a great Lesbian writer.   ISBN 0-930044-68-1   7.95

LESBIAN NUNS: BREAKING SILENCE edited by Rosemary
Curb and Nancy Manahan. 432 pp. Unprecedented autobiographies
of religious life.   ISBN 0-930044-62-2   9.95

THE SWASHBUCKLER by Lee Lynch. 288 pp. Colorful novel
set in Greenwich Village in the sixties.   ISBN 0-930044-66-5   8.95

SEX VARIANT WOMEN IN LITERATURE by Jeannette
Howard Foster. 448 pp. Literary history.   ISBN 0-930044-65-7   8.95

A HOT-EYED MODERATE by Jane Rule. 252 pp. Hard-hitting
essays on gay life; writing; art.   ISBN 0-930044-57-6   7.95

AMATEUR CITY by Katherine V. Forrest. 224 pp. A Kate
Delafield mystery. First in a series.   ISBN 0-930044-55-X   10.95

THE SOPHIE HOROWITZ STORY by Sarah Schulman. 176 pp.
Engaging novel of madcap intrigue.   ISBN 0-930044-54-1   7.95

THE YOUNG IN ONE ANOTHER'S ARMS by Jane Rule.
224 pp. Classic Jane Rule.   ISBN 0-930044-53-3   9.95

OLD DYKE TALES by Lee Lynch. 224 pp. Extraordinary stories
of our diverse Lesbian lives.   ISBN 0-930044-51-7   8.95

AGAINST THE SEASON by Jane Rule. 224 pp. Luminous,
complex novel of interrelationships.   ISBN 0-930044-48-7   8.95

LOVERS IN THE PRESENT AFTERNOON by Kathleen Fleming.
288 pp. A novel about recovery and growth.   ISBN 0-930044-46-0   8.95

TOOTHPICK HOUSE by Lee Lynch. 264 pp. Love between two
Lesbians of different classes.   ISBN 0-930044-45-2   7.95

CONTRACT WITH THE WORLD by Jane Rule. 340 pp. Powerful, panoramic novel of gay life.   ISBN 0-930044-28-2   9.95

THIS IS NOT FOR YOU by Jane Rule. 284 pp. A letter to a
beloved is also an intricate novel.   ISBN 0-930044-25-8   8.95

OUTLANDER by Jane Rule. 207 pp. Short stories and essays by
one of our finest writers.   ISBN 0-930044-17-7   8.95

These are just a few of the many Naiad Press titles — we are the oldest and largest lesbian/feminist publishing company in the world. Please request a complete catalog. We offer personal service; we encourage and welcome direct mail orders from individuals who have limited access to bookstores carrying our publications.